"Were you going to kiss me that morning?" Sarah asked, her voice slightly breathless.

Cade knew exactly what morning she was referring to. He grinned. "Did you want me to?"

She grinned back. "That's a question, not an answer. Were you?"

"Did you think I was?"

"That's still a question. Were you?"

"Maybe," he said, moving toward her.

"That's an evasive answer," she said, now truly breathless.

He stepped closer, thigh to thigh. His head lowered. "I was . . . and I am. What do you call that?"

"About time," she whispered seconds before his mouth possessed hers.

Other Second Chance at Love books by
Karen Keast

SUDDENLY THE MAGIC #225
NOTORIOUS #244

Karen Keast describes herself as "an incurable romantic who'd refuse treatment even if a cure were known." Among her favorite things are good books, the Caribbean, breathless sunsets, and rain. A resident of Shreveport, Louisiana, she shares her home with her "soft-spoken, gentle, supportive, hero-handsome" husband and two cats.

Dear Reader:

October is here—and so are the newest SECOND CHANCE AT LOVE romances!

Kelly Adams has a special talent for endowing ordinary people with extraordinary warmth and appeal. In *Sunlight and Silver* (#292), she places such thoroughly likable characters in a dramatic love story set in America's heartland, on the Mississippi River. Riverboat captain Jacy Jones comes from a long line of women who know better than to trust high-handed men. Joshua Logan comes from a privileged background of wealth and breeding that's always set him apart. The battle of wills between these two *very* independent people sparks sensual shock waves that rival the currents in the ol' Miss!

Few writers create characters as warmly human and endearingly quirky as Jeanne Grant, winner of the Romance Writers of America's Silver Medallion award. In *Pink Satin* (#293), voluptuous lingerie consultant Greer Lothrop feels more comfortable playing the role of resident housemother to new neighbor Ryan McCullough than acting the femme fatale. But Ryan isn't about to accept chicken soup in lieu of tender loving kisses. Once again, Jeanne Grant demonstrates her superlative skill as a teller of love stories in a romance you'll treasure.

With the emotional honesty and sensitivity she is fast becoming beloved for, Romance Writers of America's Bronze Medallion winner Karen Keast touches our hearts with a story of forbidden love between divorcée Sarah Braden and her ex-husband's brother, cartoonist Cade Sterling. While she never shrinks from complex emotional issues, Karen dazzles us with her skillful use of male viewpoint, her lyrical prose—*and* her humor! I can't sing the praises of Karen Keast and *Forbidden Dream* (#294) loudly enough!

Love With a Proper Stranger (#295) by Christa Merlin is a powerful love story with an element of intrigue that will keep you breathlessly turning the pages. Anya Meredith doesn't think she's a candidate for a whirlwind romance, but Brady Durant teases and tantalizes her until she impulsively surrenders to passion. Yet when Brady is linked to a mystery surrounding an antique music box, Anya's trust in her lover is severely shaken. Don't miss this gripping romance written by the author of *Kisses Incognito* (#199).

For Anglophiles everywhere, Frances Davies's frolicsome pen creates an unabashedly romantic British drawing-room comedy (at times it's a little like a French bedroom farce, too!), complete with a cast of lovable eccentrics—including the hero, dazzling romance and mystery writer Andrew Wiswood. With witty one-liners and flights of sheer poetry, Frances whisks us to heather-covered Yorkshire and immerses us in whimsy. *Fortune's Darling* (#296) is a sophisticated, delectable romp.

In *Lucky in Love* (#297) Jacqueline Topaz once again creates a bright, breezy romance that will make you feel good all over. Cheerfully unconventional exercise instructor Patti Lyon is willing to bet she can take the starch out of staunch civic leader Alex Greene. But Patti's game-show winnings and laidback lifestyle don't convince Alex to support legalized gambling. In the bedroom he's mischievously eager to play games ... but elsewhere he intends to show her there's more to life than fun and frolic!

Until next month, enjoy! Warm wishes,

Ellen Edwards

Ellen Edwards, Senior Editor
SECOND CHANCE AT LOVE
The Berkley Publishing Group
200 Madison Avenue
New York, NY 10016

Second Chance at Love

FORBIDDEN DREAM

KAREN KEAST

**SECOND CHANCE AT LOVE
BOOK**

*For Grace, who's making the angels blush
with her outrageous stories*

FORBIDDEN DREAM

First edition published October 1985

First printing

"Second Chance at Love" and the butterfly emblem are trademarks belonging to Jove Publications, Inc.

Printed in the United States of America

Second Chance at Love books are published by
The Berkley Publishing Group
200 Madison Avenue, New York, NY 10016

CHAPTER ONE

THERE WERE ONLY two things in all the world that she wanted, Sarah Braden thought wearily as she pulled into the driveway, killed the engine of the navy-blue secondhand van, and flung open the door. She wanted to forget that she had spent the last two days—twenty-eight long, gruelling hours sum total—preparing an art layout that a creatively, if not legally, blind client had just deemed unsuitable for his advertising purposes. She also wanted a gin and tonic—heavy on the gin, light on the tonic. The latter desire she viewed as a pathway to the former.

She had known it wasn't going to be easy setting herself up as a free-lance artist, she admitted, gathering up her purse and portfolio, bounding from the van, and trekking toward the house. She had known it was going to be especially difficult with her lack of experience. But for heaven's sake, wasn't it ever going to be possible to make ends meet without stretching them to the snapping point? It had been six months, six roller-coaster months, since she had left a secure job and set out on her own, and she was still struggling more than she was succeeding.

She sighed, the smell of newly mowed grass sweet-teasing her nose, and enjoyed the sudden surge of optimism that

never fled too far from her innately sunny disposition.
Brighten up, Braden. You're eating and paying your bills,
which is more than David predicted when you turned down
his offer of alimony. There'll be a way. There always is.

Leaning the leather portfolio against her leg, she wrestled
the mail from the box mounted on the front of the oyster-
white brick house, jammed the key into the lock of the door,
rattled it vigorously, and ended up shouldering open the
contrary door. She flipped on the light as she slipped inside.
Her red canvas espadrilles she kicked off near the white
wicker umbrella stand; the portfolio she angled against her
worktable, a slab of glass anchored over two sawhorses she
had painted the same spirited yellow that was splashed
throughout the small, modestly priced house the divorce
settlement had made a down payment on; her purse she
carried the few steps to the kitchen counter, where she traded
it for a glass from the overhead rack. Ice cubes clinked
while gin splashed and tonic—a sensible amount despite
her threat—diluted. Drink in hand, she crossed the room,
tugging her red blouse from her tailored khaki slacks, and
slumped onto the sofa. She levered her feet to the coffee
table and, out of sheer habit, rewound the tape of her answering machine, then depressed the playback button.

While she waited for her messages, she sipped her drink—
a cool, refreshing weapon against failure and the heat of a
Dallas August—and thumbed through her mail. She had an
electric bill that seemed somebody's idea of a bad joke, a
piece of junk mail addressed to Sarah Sterling—she marveled that there was anyone left who didn't know she was
no longer married to David Sterling—and a letter from her
sister in Louisiana. This last brought a smile to her lips in
a way that only the weekly, chatty, cheery note from her
beloved sibling could.

"Ms. Braden?" A scratchy voice suddenly erupted from
the recorder. "This is Tom Hicks down at Black Ink Press.
We've got a little problem."

"Naturally," Sarah commented sarcastically, abandoning
the mail. "What is it, Tom?" she asked as if it were perfectly

normal to carry on a conversation with one's recorded messages.

"You know the bookmark you designed for that local writer?"

"I remember."

"The one you wanted in burgundy and pink?"

"I remember, Tom," she added as her pulse did a subtle war dance in reaction to the word *problem*.

"Well, the pink is fine, but the burgundy looks more red than burgundy. I thought you might like to see it before I printed up a thousand of those little fellows. I'll be in all day tomor—" Tom Hicks's thirty seconds ended abruptly, guillotine fashion.

"Good-bye, Tom," Sarah mumbled. She brought the drink once more to her lips, rested her head on the back of the sofa, and closed her eyes. She waited to see if there'd be a second recorded message. There was.

"My name's—" The self-conscious clearing of a throat was followed again by, "My name's Frank Ambrezzi. You did some work for a friend of mine." He gave a name Sarah recognized and categorized as "menus for that new restaurant." "I was wondering if you'd be available to do some work for me. If you're interested, you can reach me at . . ." He left a number, which Sarah didn't bother to transcribe. She'd copy it from the tape later.

"You bet I'm interested, Mr. Ambrezzi," she said as she scooted her spine into an even lazier position. Her eyes were still closed, her drink still making sipping journeys to her lips.

The next caller, opting not to leave a message, had hung up, and Sarah listened to a full thirty seconds of an annoying buzz, her mind suspended somewhere between the pink/burgundy crisis and the pleasant promise of Mr. Ambrezzi. Maybe she could introduce a third color . . . Maybe Frank Ambrezzi would mean a monthly payment on the van . . .

The buzzing ended. Silence. Sarah shifted, sending the ice cubes in the glass into a clatter-dance. She dreamily wondered if there would be another message or if she'd played out the last of the afternoon's phone activity. She had just opened her mouth on an indelicate yawn when the recorder once again sparked to life.

"Hey, Sunshine..."

Sarah's mouth closed, and her eyes flew open. She eased her feet to the floor and sat upright. The gin and tonic she abandoned to a cork coaster on the coffee table.

"...don't you ever answer your phone?" The voice was male, all male, the words spoken with all the haste of warm honey crawling down the slope of a sun-showered sand dune. "When you light somewhere"—Sarah could almost see the smile at the speaking lips—"you want to call me? I need to talk with you." He left his number. "Oh, and call collect." A fumbling of the receiver, as if the caller was about to hang up, skittered across the line. At the last moment he reconsidered. "I've missed you, Sunshine," he added huskily.

The recorder went blank, and just as blankly Sarah punched the off-button. For several seconds she sat staring at the mute machine. Slowly, a wave of pleasure began to lap at her consciousness, and she whispered a single word that seemed to fill the empty room. "Cade."

The past flashed at her with blitzkrieg speed. "Cade Sterling, I'd like you to meet Sarah Braden, within the hour to be Mrs. David Sterling. Sweetheart, I'd like you to meet my best man"—here a smile had taken possession of David Sterling's perfectly shaped mouth—"and my little brother."

The "little brother," who'd cut short a business trip in New York in order to attend the hurry-up wedding, had turned out to be five years younger than David, fourteen months younger than Sarah. He had also turned out to be brawnier than David, a muscle-packed, thick-shouldered, football build compared to David's slightly taller basketball physique. Cade's sky-blue eyes contrasted with David's dark brown ones, while Cade's hair, brown like his brother's but lighter, pitted the shade of summer-dried grass against the color of deeply roasted coffee. Both men were handsome and appealing, David in a brooding sort of way, Cade in an open, I've-got-all-my-cards-on-the-table way. Though she hadn't known it at the time, Cade Sterling's first words to her had been prophetic.

"You don't really want to marry my renegade brother, do you?" he had asked, his eyes twinkling with the teasing blue fire of devilment. As it turned out, she would have been better off not marrying David Sterling, but it had taken her two long, miserable years to arrive at that conclusion.

Sarah played back the recording, hastily jotted down Cade Sterling's phone number, and at his repeated words, the gentle wave of pleasure she'd felt minutes before crested to a joy-tipped swell that threatened to tumble her headfirst into happiness. It had been a year and a half since she'd seen him or heard his voice, six months since she'd received his note wishing her success in her new business venture. She'd missed him. Until now she hadn't realized just how much. And why shouldn't she have missed him? she asked herself as she reached for the phone. Wasn't he the best brother-in-law in the world? The best friend she'd had in all her thirty-one years?

She dialed the out-of-town number. The phone began to ring, its mechanical chiming interspersed with crystal-clear memory-scenes from the past.

Ring.

"They took it, Sarah!" Cade had said, his excited voice coming to her over a span of three years that seemed more like three minutes. "They took my cartoon strip. 'Rigby Rat' is going to be syndicated all over the country."

"That's wonderful! Marvelous!" she had bubbled into the phone. "Why didn't David tell me?"

After the slightest pause he'd answered, "I haven't told David. I wanted you to be the first to know."

Ring.

"Why do you call me Sunshine?" she had asked over a chess game they'd played one evening when David was once again working late. "It can't be my sunny tresses," she teased, tunneling her fingers through hair as black as the obsidian chessmen before her.

He had maneuvered his knight, pronouncing "Check"

before raising his eyes to hers. "Because you make the world a brighter place."

She immediately counterattacked with her stately bishop. "Checkmate," she announced softly, looking up at him again and adding, "Is the world so dark?"

"Sometimes," he had answered, his eyes shading from light to the blue obscurity of oceans deep and asleep.

Ring.

Sarah frowned and transferred the phone to her other ear. Why didn't he answer? And what did he need to talk to her about? She hoped nothing was wrong. She also wondered, and far from the first time, why she'd heard so little—one note only—from him since she and David had separated and divorced. Now, as always, she was forced to settle for the answer that blood was, indeed, thicker than water, that being a brother took precedence over being a brother-in-law. Especially when the two brothers were as close as Cade and David.

Ring.

The phone sounded snatched from its cradle. "Hello?" came a slightly breathless greeting.

"Hey, Sterling, don't you ever answer your phone?" she teased, tossing back his own words.

Sarah had begun to fear she had a wrong number when she heard a drawled, "Well, well, if it isn't that famous free-lance artist from Big D, Texas."

She laughed. Lord, it was good to hear him in the flesh! "It's that *hungry* free-lance artist from Dallas," she corrected.

She heard the amusement drain from his voice. "Are things that bad?"

"Only kidding," she hastened to add. "Although I wouldn't find a few more clients objectionable."

"Good. Glad to hear that," he answered.

Sarah leaned back, lifting the phone from the table onto the sofa with her. She once again propped up her feet. "Your sensitivity, Sterling, is overwhelming," she said, easily falling back into their comfortable, playful banter. Like the flash of a firefly, it flitted through her mind that she no longer felt as tired as she had minutes before.

"How are you?" he asked seriously. "I mean, how are you really? Except for starving to death, of course."

"I'm fine, really. I'm working hard, but I love what I'm doing. And I am managing to keep afloat."

"It'll get easier. Free-lancing is always spotty at first."

"Tell me about it," she quipped as she coiled the cord around her finger.

"How're your parents and your sister?" he asked.

Sarah smiled. "Dad's threatening for the fourth time to retire, and Mom is scared to death he means it this time. She doesn't want him to cut into her soap operas. She's afraid she'll go from watching 'The Young and the Restless' to living with 'The Old and the Restless.'" Her smile broadened. "And Terri is great. She has another baby. A little boy."

"That makes one of each, doesn't it?"

"Yeah. Denise and Daniel."

"That's wonderful. Tell her I said congratulations."

"I will, but listen, how are you?" She started to add that it had been a long time since she'd heard from him, but she decided against it. She wasn't exactly sure why.

"As old Rigby Rat would say, I'm as fine as a wartless frog on a polished lily pad."

Sarah laughed with mirth and pride. Like thousands of people across the country, she started every day with the comic strip depicting the adventures—more often the mis-adventures—of Rigby Rat, a muskrat constantly and humorously on the run from trappers and one amorous female muskrat named Ms. Mona. The comic strip was wise and funny and had that intangible something that had nudged it right into the hearts of its readers. Its success was due *in toto* to the talent, creativity, and sensitivity of the man now speaking.

"Hey, you didn't call collect!"

"I can spring for a long-distance call." An impish smile played at her lips. "I just won't eat tomorrow."

"Dammit!"

"I'm only kidding! Honest!"

"Hang up, and I'll call you right back," he ordered.

"I will not!"

"Okay, I'll just have the charges reversed."

"You will not, Cade Sterling."

"Sunshine . . ."

"If you don't start talking, I won't be able to eat for *two* days," she said, unable to resist another bit of teasing.

He muttered an unflattering remark about her stubbornness, on the heels of which he threw in, "You want to work for me?"

The abrupt question caught her off guard, and her eyes widened. "What?"

"Do you want to work for me? I need an artist to draw the strip for the next six to eight weeks, maybe longer."

Sarah fidgeted with a button of her blouse. "But I don't know anything about cartooning."

"What's there to know? You can draw. All you really need to do is recreate the figures I've already created. I'd still do the word copy."

He went on to explain everything the job would entail, including the fact that it would be best, since the project would require for the most part daily execution, if she moved into his house in Gilmer. He concluded by mentioning a sum of money so large it made Sarah's head swim like only four gin and tonics could. Absently, she reached for her drink and swallowed once as he was pointing out that she could bring her other work with her—the comic strip wouldn't demand all her time—and that she could have her calls forwarded if she was afraid of losing new projects. And making the two-hour trip back to Dallas to meet with clients, he pointed out, wouldn't be that big a hardship. He reminded her that Gilmer was located in east Texas, not at the end of the earth. Sarah took another sip of her drink, hardly tasting it.

"Interested?" he asked at the end of his recruitment recital.

"I don't know," she answered truthfully, her mind still numb at the prospect.

"Look, Sunshine . . ." The words trailed off to a muffled thud. A groan and a harsh expletive followed.

"What is it?" she asked in concern. "What's wrong?"

"I can't get used to the damned cast, and I just rammed it into the kitchen cabinet," he muttered.

"Cast?" she asked, sitting up suddenly. "What cast?"

"Didn't I mention my broken wrist?"

Sarah's eyes rolled heavenward. "No, you did not. I would have remembered."

"Well, I broke my wrist. No big deal."

"And it's your drawing hand, right?" she asked intuitively.

"What else?" he wisecracked. "So are you going to do your good deed for the day and help out an injured man? Or am I going to have to bury my pride and beg? Burying is going to be wretchedly difficult for a one-handed man."

Sarah hesitated.

"I'm going to have to beg, huh?" he asked, his words spiced with amusement.

"No, it's just . . ."

It was just what? she asked herself. He was offering her a wonderful job opportunity, to be part, albeit temporarily, of an award-winning, nationally syndicated cartoon. That wouldn't look bad on her résumé. Not bad at all. And he wasn't asking her to give up her other free-lance assignments; in fact, he was encouraging her to accept more. And the money he was offering—that alone should have her breaking the speed limit all the way from Dallas to Gilmer. Oh, Lord, imagine knowing where *several* van payments were coming from. Imagine some new clothes. Imagine a steak and a baked potato with all the trimmings instead of tuna fish three nights a week. And the bottom line was, he needed her. A good friend needed her. So why was she hesitating?

"SOS . . . Mayday . . ." she heard him say.

She swallowed hard and ran her fingers through her short

black hair. She knew why she was hesitating. She knew exactly why. What had happened the last time they were together had left her, if not shaken, at least buffeted by emotional tremors. Not that anything had *really* happened. A chaste kiss between friends was hardly sinful. She knew Cade would be shocked to discover that she had remembered that Sunday afternoon kiss all these many months; she was certain it would never again cross his mind. But for some reason she couldn't clearly fathom, the memory of the kiss had stayed with her, and she wondered time and again what it would be like to face him once more. The idea both intrigued and frightened her, and it was now causing her to hesitate.

"Help?" he added with a melodramatic flourish that would have made her laugh had not the single word sent her painfully hurtling back in time.

"Help me!" she had sobbed into the receiver that faraway Saturday night. "Please help me! It's the baby!" Another cry had racked her body. "Oh, God, I think I'm losing my baby!"

"Take it easy," Cade had soothed, though his voice had been shot through with concern and thinly throttled panic. "Where's David?"

"I don't know. I called his office . . ."

Sarah would always remember the violence with which Cade had uttered the basest of profanities. "I'll be right there. Hang on, Sunshine. Just hang on."

Minutes later, he had raced through the Dallas streets en route to Parkland Memorial Hospital. Most of the trip he had driven with one hand; the other had been securely laced with hers.

"I owe you one," she said with a tremulous smile as they screeched to a halt at the emergency entrance. "I—" Her next words had died around a moan and the sharp pain tearing through her abdomen.

"Sunshine?" came a voice from the present. "Are you there?"

She roused herself from the dark past and moved her

hand from the flat of her stomach, where it had unconsciously gone in bitter remembrance. She owed Cade. Owed him a debt she could never repay. She'd needed him; he'd unhesitatingly come. Now he had asked for her help. She needed no other motivation.

"When do you want me?"

She wasn't certain, but she thought she heard a relieved sigh travel through the line. "Tomorrow? My deadlines just don't stop coming."

"I can be there by late afternoon."

"Great!" He paused. "Thanks, Sarah."

She smiled. "You're welcome. I'm looking forward to meeting Rigby Rat personally."

Cade laughed and proceeded to give her instructions to his house, adding, "Drive carefully, huh?"

"I will. See you tomorrow," she said and started to hang up.

He stopped her at the last second. "Sarah, are your eyes still gray?"

The unexpected question startled her, but her momentary astonishment soon gave way to a burst of giggles. "No, I traded them in for blue."

His smile traversed the miles. "I'll bet it was a lousy trade," he said seconds before he severed the connection.

Sarah stared at the buzzing receiver, then slid it back into place. Her lips were still wreathed in a smile, and her spirits were high, if a little uncertain, at the prospect of seeing Cade again. He was her friend. A dear friend. And she had missed him.

As she stood and walked toward the kitchen, a sudden thought came to her. She hadn't once asked about David. The truth was, she realized with some surprise, he hadn't even entered her mind.

Ninety miles away, Cade Sterling's hand slipped from the wall phone. He was uncertain just how long his fingers had been gripping the plastic. Lowering his arm to his side, he leaned against the kitchen cabinet and took a deep breath.

How could he have been so wrong? He had thought he remembered every nuance of her voice—he had worked so hard to hold on to that precious memory—but the moment she had spoken, he had realized what crude impostors his memories were. Crude, inadequate, frail replicas of the warmth and womanly sound of Sarah Braden. Which led him to wonder now just how accurate were his visual images of her, images he'd zealously clung to in the long, lonely stretches of more than five hundred dark nights.

As if summoned by command, her image flashed before his eyes. She lay pale and still with the loss of her child—David's child. Her eyes shone through a mist of tears and medication, yet they possessed a dignity that, even now, tapped a feeling in him he'd never before known. And then, that dignity still in place, she'd calmly announced that she had asked for a divorce. He hadn't been surprised at the announcement. His reaction, however, had surprised him. He hadn't intended to kiss her. It had just happened. Ten seconds of a sublime magic that had changed his life. For with her mouth soft and pliant and alluringly vulnerable against his, he had admitted what he'd known all along: He was in love with his brother's wife.

Cade swore quietly and reached for the now warm can of beer that stood forgotten on the cabinet. He took a long, slow swallow. One fact hadn't changed. He was still in love with Sarah. One other fact had changed, however. She was no longer married to his brother. This latter fact opened up a world of possibilities. He'd see her tomorrow, he'd look his fill of her, he'd love her, and he'd wait. And maybe, maybe, when the time was right and if he hadn't used up all the luck this life offered, he'd make her love him.

By nine o'clock the next morning, Sarah had packed, called her sister to tell her where she could be reached in the weeks to come, and arranged with a neighbor to forward her mail and phone messages to Gilmer.

"Don't you worry about a thing," said Alma Babish, a mother hen of a woman who clucked out commands so swiftly it put her retired drill sergeant husband to shame. "Give me that address again. Ah, dang it! Hand me that pen, will you?" she said, throwing down the one in her hand and snatching up the one Sarah offered. "Explain to me how a brand-new pen can be out of ink." Waiting for no response, she forged ahead with, "Now give me that address." The words were barely out of Sarah's mouth when Mrs. Babish pounced with another command. "Tell me if I've got this right. Twice a week I'm to transcribe messages from your answering machine and send them, along with your mail, to this Gilmer address."

"Right," Sarah assured her, suddenly wishing she'd gotten an answering machine with a remote call-in unit.

"How long will you be gone?"

"Six to eight weeks. I'm not really sure."

One of the woman's salt-and-pepper eyebrows rose in an uncanny facsimile of a moralistic question mark. "And you'll be staying up there alone with this cartoonist?"

"He's my brother-in-law," Sarah explained, stifling a smile as well as a funny warm feeling evoked by the word *alone*.

"Oh, I didn't realize he was family," Mrs. Babish said, dropping the suddenly uninteresting subject and charging ahead. "Don't you worry about a thing here. Oh, better give me your key. Have you called your parents? Have you stopped your paper? Show me how this machine works. Now you call me if I can do anything else. Promise you will."

When Sarah was allowed to speak, she did promise. Moments later Mrs. Babish departed, leaving Sarah feeling relieved to have the matter settled and a little punch-drunk from all the imperatives it had taken to settle it.

By noon she had made a decision regarding the troublesome pink and burgundy bookmark and had met with Mr. Frank Ambrezzi. Sarah had assured him she could do the artwork for the advertising campaign he envisioned for his chain of yogurt shops. He hired her on the spot.

Taking a needed break, she stopped for a lunch of hamburger, fries, and diet cola. As she dragged a french fry through a puddle of ketchup, she thought back to her sister's reaction at learning she was on her way to work for Cade. After a slight pause, Terri Richards had gushed with pleasure. It was the pause Sarah didn't quite know how to interpet. Now, four hours later, as she plopped the crisp sliver of potato into her mouth, she shrugged and admitted she'd probably imagined the whole thing. After all, what could possibly be wrong in working for Cade? It was just as Mrs. Babish had said: He was family.

Sarah dashed from the fast-food restaurant to an appointment with another prospective client. She shouldn't have hurried. The interview went poorly. The woman seemed uncertain of her needs, unsure of Sarah's ability to fulfill them should they magically be discovered, and unwilling to listen to any of Sarah's suggestions. When Sarah left the woman's office, she knew she'd seen the last of her—with any luck.

Toward the end of the afternoon, as she was preparing to head the van in the direction of Gilmer, Sarah impulsively whipped into the parking lot of Prestonwood Mall. She gave herself a pep talk as she parked the van and made her way to the stores. It was the middle of August, right? August meant summer sales, right? And wasn't she about to earn some extra money? And hadn't it been ages since she'd pampered herself with anything new? The questions led to the desired answer.

Within the hour she had purchased, all at reduced prices, a pair of navy shorts, a coordinating plaid shirt, a black and ecru skirt, and a pair of sandals that looped twice about her shapely ankles and tied. As a result of the shopping spree, Sarah felt great as she climbed back into the van. Target: Gilmer. Target: Rigby Rat. Target: Cade Sterling.

She soon left behind the snarl of city traffic, and the interstate stretched before her in all its gray and monotonous glory, the yellow median line beckoning mesmerically. The rich black Texas soil she sped by was patchworked against spreads of sun-bleached grass, graduating from shades of straw to dun, while lofty trees—pine, oak, lacy elm, and nameless others—huddled in green groves as if seeking protection from the vastness. Cows grazed; an occasional oil well pumped; billboards pleaded their propaganda. Shading her eyes with sunglasses, Sarah turned on the radio, adjusted her hips more comfortably in the seat, and settled back to make highway time.

About thirty-five miles from her destination, she glanced over at the sacked purchases on the seat beside her. Funny, she mused, reaching over and rattling a bag open to peek inside, that it sometimes took so little to delight the feminine heart. But her smile was tempered by sadness as she reflected that not too long ago she could have made these same purchases with little concern about their price. In fact, she could have doubled her acquisitions and never batted an eye. David Sterling had never been selfish with his money. He had been selfish only with himself.

She hadn't even suspected—though, looking back, perhaps she should have—David's flawed personality. But then, she thought bitterly, how much could you learn about another person in a mere six weeks? Although she'd never been prone to flighty behavior, David Sterling had swept her off her feet and thrust her head into billowy clouds. From the first moment she'd met him at a party, he had fascinated her with his good looks, his interesting talk, and his ability to be both present and absent at the same time. Perhaps this elusiveness only underscored his desirability, making every woman want to be the one to capture his undivided attention. Wherever the blame was to be laid, and whatever the blame was to be, she had fallen helplessly, happily in love. David had echoed her sentiment and asked her to marry him. She had unhesitatingly agreed.

A few months into the marriage, she had suspected problems. A year into the marriage she was quite certain of their existence. It seemed that one of anything was never enough for her new husband. He worked long hours, maintaining two businesses. They owned two homes—one a lovely split-level brick in Dallas suburbia, the other a rustic but charming cabin on Ray Hubbard Lake, some thirty minutes' drive from the first. More and more often, "business" occasions arose in which David worked late into the night or sometimes all night long. More and more often, Sarah began to suspect that something other than business was involved. A year and a half into the shaky marriage, a tube of lipstick in a shade Sarah didn't wear confirmed her suspicions. Her husband was seeing other women, at the lake cabin. Apparently, the unsatisfying number "one" had again fallen prey to the excitement and fulfillment of two or more.

Sarah eased up on the van's cruise control and accelerated around a car that had passed her minutes before and then slowed down to an irritating creep.

But she'd give David one thing, she thought, resetting the cruise control. He hadn't denied his indiscretions when she hurled them at him. He admitted right up front that he was guilty. And that he was wrong, that he shouldn't have desecrated their vows. He also admitted that he wasn't certain why he had done so. Sarah, though no psychologist, had by now arrived at her own conclusion. Though projecting supreme confidence, David Sterling was burdened, she believed, with an underlying insecurity, an insecurity that caused him to hedge his business bets with a backup occupation, an insecurity that needed the constant reinforcement of feminine attraction. Perversely, his reticence kept him from giving of himself fully to anyone. He wasn't a bad man, nor really a weak one; he was simply a man with a . . . with a flaw. He had asked her to stay with him, to forgive him. She had suggested counseling; he had reluctantly agreed. She stayed, and she watched as he postponed therapy, one anemic excuse chaining itself to another. She had no idea whether he was still seeing other women; she didn't want to know—and she considered that her flaw. It was easier to close her eyes.

Into this unsettling scene came the fact that she was pregnant. She concentrated body and soul on the life she carried within her. David became shadowy, the child bright in a sunstorm of golden light. And into this light also stepped Cade Sterling.

He became a friend, a companion, a diversion against lonely times, and though she never spoke to him of marital problems—never even hinted of them—she often wondered if Cade sensed how unhappy she was and why. At times she thought he did, though he never gave any sign of it. The two brothers were close, the kind of close that came from having no other family. Cade would never jeopardize that relationship by intruding in his brother's marriage, and Sarah didn't expect him to. It was enough for her that they played an occasional chess game, shared an occasional laugh, spent an occasional quiet evening together when David was running his usual late or no-show.

And then one Saturday night she lost the baby.

It was Cade's, not her husband's, words of comfort she heard when she woke to the sterile white of hospital and dashed hopes. It was Cade who held her while she cried. It was Cade who listened to her incoherent, tear-racked ramblings. Cade who soothed her heartache with tenderly crooned words. And Cade who told her there would be other babies. But even in her groggy state, Sarah knew that there would be no more babies by David Sterling.

The moment David was found—she never asked where—she had demanded a divorce.

The next day when Cade stopped by the hospital, she told him of her decision. He had said nothing; he had simply pulled her into the shelter of his arms. Neither had spoken. She had felt no need to justify herself; he had obviously felt no need to hear her justification. And then he had kissed her, briefly, fleetingly, merely the silken touch of warm male lips against hers. It had been only a brotherly kiss of solace, a kiss between special friends.

And yet.

And yet it had stayed in her mind to haunt and tease, and sometimes in the darkest of the nights, when dreams and wishes and suppressed desires claimed their momentary freedom, she would relive it with such vividness that she would suddenly be overwhelmed by the inappropriateness of her thoughts. Just as she was right now.

With gratitude she saw the sign announcing the small, sleepy town of Gilmer, population 5,119, and she gladly relinquished her thoughts to safer ones. She checked the instructions Cade had given her and, briefly wondering why he had given up city life for so rural a location, pointed the van down a dirt road a couple of miles out of town. In the swirl of dust, in the smell of country, in the crackly hot feel of the blistering summer sun, Sarah abandoned all thoughts of the past, all thoughts of any imagined improprieties, and simply opened herself to feelings: the excitement of a new adventure, the security of a solid job, the pleasure of soon seeing a good friend.

Seconds later, she made the last gentle turn in the road and brought the van to a halt. Her gaze shifted to the house, a beautiful brown and beige stone structure actually set into the sloping hillside. The Texas earth, alive with green grass and dainty spikes of purple verbena, acted as a roof, leaving the impression that land and house had entered into a magical singularity. Lovely, Sarah thought as her eyes took in the unusual scene.

She eased from the van, walked a short distance, and stepped into the recessed entryway. Shaded coolness wrapped itself around her as she pushed her sunglasses to the top of her head.

She rang the doorbell and waited, studying the gigantic pot of fern cascading regally by the front door. And she was suddenly gripped by a breathless feeling of anticipation. And panic.

What if he'd changed in the last year and a half since she'd seen him? What if their relationship was now awkward, not the comfortable camaraderie they'd once shared? What if . . .

The door swung open. Sarah's head jerked up, her eyes instantly meeting Cade's. Warm eyes. Peaceful, serene eyes. Eyes clear and bright and a come-hither blue. A thatch of wheat-colored hair fell over his forehead, giving him a roguish, mature look at the same time it lent youthfulness to his twenty-nine years. Eyebrows, full and bushy and

rambling in an appealing lack of design, matched the golden
hue of lush, thick, indecently sweeping lashes. Barefoot,
he wore white tennis shorts and a Dallas Cowboys T-shirt.
The white cast immobilizing his right wrist and hand contrasted markedly with the bronze of sunbeamed skin.

And then it happened.

He smiled.

At the simple, lazy arc of his lips, Sarah's world shifted
on its foundation. Suddenly the man before her was no
longer the Cade Sterling she'd known. This Cade Sterling
wasn't the talented creator of "Rigby Rat." This Cade Sterling wasn't her friend, her confidant, her comrade. This
Cade Sterling wasn't her brother-in-law. For the first time,
the man before her was simply . . . a man. A handsome man,
a sensual man. A man who had just sent her pulse to the
furthermost reaches of fast.

CHAPTER TWO

THE REACTION CAME so swiftly, was so unbidden and so powerful, that her defenses had no time to marshal themselves. The surge of her pulse tailgated the thinning of her breath, and rushed a faint blush to her cheeks.

Sanity surfaced, and she shoved the startling response to a mind corner where she could study it later—should she become brave enough. She forced a smile to her lips.

Something equally potent had flashed in Cade's eyes, casting them a deep, velvety blue, but it disappeared just as quickly as it had appeared. His smile widened.

"You lied," he teased. "You still have gray eyes."

She felt the tension recede and heard her own laughter. He stepped back, letting her in. Careful not to engage his injured wrist, he eased his left arm around her and pulled her against his chest in a snug half hug.

"Damn, it's good to see you," he said, his breath warm against her cheek.

At their bodies' contact, she stiffened momentarily, but then gave herself up to the familiar feel of the old Cade Sterling. This man was not the stranger of moments before. This man was her friend, her brother-in-law. This man was her safe harbor in the flaring storm. She draped both arms about his wide back and, closing her eyes, returned his hug.

"It's good to see you, too," she replied honestly.

The embrace was long and heartfelt.

"Let me look at you," he said, pulling back. His gaze traveled every inch between black hair and navy shoes. "You look great," he pronounced.

"You look great," she said simultaneously.

They both laughed.

"How's your wrist?" she asked, glancing down at the plaster cast.

His eyes dipped briefly before again meeting hers. "Oh, it's fine," he answered, blithely changing the subject. "How was the trip?"

"No problem."

"Did you have any trouble finding the house?"

"Came right to it."

"Great. I—" A ping sounded somewhere off to the right. "That's the timer. My brownies are done."

"Brownies?" she asked, raising an eyebrow. "I'm impressed."

"Don't be," he answered with a smile. "I cheated. They came in a doughy package, and you just smear them into a pan." Turning, he padded toward the kitchen. "Be right back," he called over his shoulder.

"I love your house," she shouted after him as she removed her sunglasses and laid them and her purse on the pecan-colored coffee table.

"Thanks," he shouted in return. "Why don't you look around?"

She did—and immediately fell in love. Expecting a home buried in the earth to be dark, dank, and dreary, she was pleasantly surprised. Strategically placed skylights admitted the setting sun, bathing the room in an orange and gold glow. A nutmeg-brown terrazzo floor, dotted with rugs, apparently ran the extent of the house, which seemed to be in the shape of a doughnut, the hole being a patio filled with lush greenery and comfortable-looking white furniture. The living room, done in blending shades of beige, royal blue, and persimmon, was pretty yet masculine and exuded silence and privacy, peace and serenity. Sarah thought it suited its owner.

She was staring up at the diamond-shaped skylight above the plaid sofa when some noise caught her attention. She glanced toward its source. Cade, who had slipped into a pair of thonged sandals, leaned against a doorjamb, his broad shoulders, legs generously dusted in brown hair, and striking face creating a study in negligent attractiveness. Something in his nonchalant stance suggested he might have been standing there for a while.

Sarah directed her gaze back to the skylight, attributing the sudden skip in her heartbeat to the long, tiring day. "Can you see the stars at night?" she asked.

Pushing from the jamb in a single easy motion, he started across the room. "Sure. If you special order them."

"Could we do that?" she asked, smiling at him.

"Consider it done."

Their eyes met. She wondered why she had never realized before how really handsome Cade was. Or had she? Sarah pulled her gaze away and tucked a hand into the back pocket of her jeans. "Your house is beautiful. At least what I've seen."

"Thanks."

"I had no idea you were interested in earth-sheltered homes. You never mentioned wanting to build one."

He shrugged his broad shoulders. "I'd always toyed with the idea. A year and a half ago seemed a good time to do it."

His eyes melded once more with hers, almost daring her to ask what was so significant about a year and a half ago. The question did cross her mind, but she couldn't quite work up the nerve to ask it. Nerve? Why should asking the question involve nerve?

He smiled suddenly. "Hungry?"

The troublesome thought vanished, and she pursed her mouth in contemplation. Nodding her head, she said, "I think I am. Lunch was a long way down the road, literally and figuratively."

"Let's collect your things from the car and get you settled

in," he said as he started for the front door. She fell into step beside him. "How does dinner at seven sound?" he asked, draping his arm across her shoulders the same way he had hundreds of times before. And just as she had done hundreds of times before, she slipped her hand around the slim curve of his waist.

"Sounds great," she answered.

"How about each man—" He grimaced. "Oops! How about each person for himself or herself for breakfast and lunch, but we take turns cooking dinner?"

"Sounds fair," she agreed. Then she cast up suspicious eyes. "You can cook, can't you, Sterling?"

"Can I cook?" he huffed, feigning offense and adding Rigby Rat's current catchphrase, "Is a swamp gooey with 'gators?"

Sarah laughed and tightened her hold about his waist. She was still uncertain of the hands into which she was placing her nutrition, but it really didn't matter. Peanut butter and jelly with Cade would be better than a feast with any king.

Fifteen minutes later, with the teasing comment that he could have moved to Outer Mongolia with half the luggage she'd brought, Cade left Sarah at the door to the bedroom that would be hers for the duration of her stay. Dinner would be ready in thirty minutes. He told her to holler if she needed anything.

She didn't. The bedroom, with its adjoining half bath, both done in powder-blue and white, boasted everything she could possibly need. Cade had anticipated her every whim, from fresh towels laid out near the frosted glass shower stall to a bed already turned back, revealing crisp white sheets trimmed in eyelet embroidery that looked suspiciously as if they'd been newly purchased with a female in mind. A bunch of daisies, white with butter-yellow centers, bloomed on a cherry-wood desk. Sarah smiled at the slightly askew arrangement in an overly large crystal beer stein and savored the warm feeling that was making her its welcome prisoner.

The warm feeling lasted all through her shower. As she turned off the faucets, stepped from the glass cubicle, and reached for a blue towel, she heard the continuing splatter of water. Cade, too, was taking a shower. Obviously right next door. Which probably meant his bedroom wasn't far away. The thought of sharing a house with Cade, with all the intimacies that implied—unexpected peeks at her nightgown, knowing he slept and dreamed only feet away from her, seeing each other first thing in the morning without benefit of makeup or good moods—unsettled her. She told herself she'd feel the same with any man. She even believed it.

When she heard the running water stop and the muted clang of a shower door sliding open, an image of a wet, nude Cade flashed in Sarah's mind. Before she could stop herself, she wondered if the golden-brown hair she'd often seen peeping out of the V of his shirt matted his chest as heavily as his brother's did. And if so, did that hair disappear into a thin, tapering line that intersected his navel and stopped just short of his . . . Sarah halted the renegade thought and hastened into the bedroom to dress, telling herself she needed to hurry. This she didn't bother to believe.

Both showers dripped, the tranquil splat of Cade's answered by the soothing spatter of Sarah's.

Drip . . . drip-drop . . . drip . . . drip-drop. Above the sound, for the sensitive ears of dreamers only, rose yet another murmur of water, this the gentle furrowing of a pond's smooth surface.

"She came," the feminine muskrat voice intoned, the words mingling with summer breeze and birdsong.

"Of course she came," the male muskrat answered, his reply battling the hum of mosquitoes and the throaty croak of a squat green frog.

"What happens next?"

"Patience, Mona. You must learn muskrat patience."

The voices faded, drowned out in the pond's mur-

*muring purl of water. In the tranquil splat of water.
In the soothing spatter of water. In the water's* drip
. . . drip-drop.

At one minute after seven, Sarah, dressed in her new
skirt and sandals, stepped into the persimmon-and-beige
kitchen. Copper pans, as shiny as newly minted pennies,
hung above a wooden butcher block, and a small dining
table, laid with two attractive place settings, sat at the kitch-
en's end. Light bounced cheerily off richly paneled walls
and several hanging baskets of ivy.

"Mmm. Something smells good."

Cade stood at the stove, his left hand awkwardly paddling
a wooden spoon back and forth in a thick red sauce. His
right hand he held even more awkwardly at his side. He
looked up at the sound of her voice and smiled.

"Hope you like spaghetti."

"Love it."

He ladled out a small amount of the sauce, pursed his
lips and blew on it, then aimed the spoon at Sarah's mouth.
She eagerly took his offering. "Mmm. It *is* good," she said,
licking her lips.

"It should be," he replied, laying down the spoon. "I
worked a full ninety seconds getting it out of a jar."

Sarah laughed. "I thought the recipe tasted remarkably
like mine."

"The spaghetti sauce manufacturers and I have an
arrangement," Cade said as he tested the long strands of
pasta for doneness. "I don't make spaghetti sauce, and they
don't draw comic strips. So far, it's working out real well."

Sarah laughed again.

"I've missed your laugh," Cade said softly, seriously.

"And I've missed your making me laugh," she returned
with the same softness, the same seriousness. On some
subliminal level, she filed away the fact that his hair was
still slightly damp from the shower and that he had a clean
smell accented subtly with a spicy after shave.

For long moments they watched each other.

"Let's eat, huh?" he said, finally tearing his eyes from hers.

"Let's eat," she agreed.

"If you'll take the spaghetti, I'll get the salad and French bread," he offered.

Sarah watched as he moved toward the refrigerator. His athletically taut legs, encased in white slacks, moved with a simple grace; his muscles rippled beneath his plaid shirt as he wrenched open the refrigerator door and reached in for the salad. He straightened to a height just shy of six feet, closed the door with a bump of his hip, and juggled the bowl between good hand and bad. She saw him grimace from that effort.

"Does your wrist hurt?" she asked.

"Not too bad."

"How did you break it?" With two scorched potholders she carried the steaming pasta to the sink, where she began to drain it. Cade, having settled the salad on the table, was following suit with grated cheese and hot garlic bread.

"Don't ask."

Through the steam billowing up from the sink, she cast a quick look in his direction. "How?" When he didn't answer, she prompted, "Cade?"

He looked over at her and gave a sheepish grin that made him look all boy, all man. "I fell out of bed," he answered, quickly adding, "I'd appreciate it if you wouldn't laugh."

Sarah's face remained stonily bland. Then her lips twitched, and she hastily turned away to busy herself at the sink.

"You're laughing," he accused.

"I'm not. Honest, I'm not," she denied, trying to suppress the smile by biting the insides of her cheeks. But the smile was intent on bursting forth, which it did. "You fell out of bed?" she asked incredulously as she turned around again.

Cade was having a hard time keeping his own lips from curving. "That's right."

"How, in heaven's name, do you fall out of bed?" she asked, her smile widening.

"Believe me, it's easy. All you have to do is turn over while you're groggy, misjudge the distance to the edge of the bed, and plop, the next thing you know, you're on the floor with a sharp pain in your wrist. Actually, the falling isn't all that bad. It's the landing that gets you."

Sarah made a sound between a titter and a cough.

"I'll have you know the doctor said that tumbling out of bed isn't all that uncommon." Cade's smile finally erupted, matching hers. "Of course, he said that right after he laughed."

With that, Sarah gave up the struggle and her laughter filled the kitchen. It was obviously an irresistible siren, for Cade, though he tried not to, was forced to join her.

"Are you telling me the truth?" she asked when the laughter died away and she had wiped a tear from her eye. "Did you really fall out of bed? Or is this just an example of your creative imagination?"

"Honest to God. And I hadn't even been drinking. And to make matters really ridiculous, I'd played a hard game of rugby just the evening before without a scratch."

Sarah's eyebrows rose. "Rugby?"

"You know, British football."

"So super-jock played a hard game of rugby and came home and fell out of his bed?" A smile still played at her lips.

"That's about the size of it," he answered, heading for the cabinet. "Damned embarrassing, isn't it?"

"You obviously need someone to—" She paused. She had been on the verge of saying that he obviously needed someone to take care of him, but for some reason she resisted the image of some woman doing precisely that.

"Need someone to what?" he asked, smothering the spaghetti in sauce and handing her a plate. His eyes briefly grazed hers.

"You need someone to install bedrails," she supplied. "Here, let me have those," she offered, taking both plates and carrying them to the table.

"You don't think bedrails will hurt my macho image?"

"What macho image?" she teased.

"That was low, Braden. Real low."

Sarah glanced up. Cade was looking at her. They were both smiling.

"I have another confession," he said a few moments later.

"Yeah? Anything as good as the last one?"

"This one falls into the category of serious. We don't have any wine. We're going to have to settle for milk."

"What? No wine?" she said with a dramatic gasp.

"Told you it was serious."

A warmth settled in her eyes. "I think we can handle milk. I'll get it." While she removed the carton from the refrigerator, Cade took out two glasses. As she poured the milk, Sarah suddenly giggled.

"Is that giggle aimed at my mishap in bed or my macho image?"

"Neither," she answered. "You remember that time we killed that bottle of French rosé while we played chess?"

"Remember? It's not every day you get to see your opponent checkmate her own king."

"I *was* a little tipsy," she avowed, placing both glasses on the table.

"A little? Lady, you were out of it, as in intoxicated, inebriated, sloshed."

Sarah's hand flew to her hips in feigned indignation. "You weren't much better, Sterling. It took you a full two minutes to realize your king was safe and sound. And by then, you'd cleared half the chess board and were demanding a rematch."

Cade was grinning. Then Sarah watched as his grin slowly disappeared.

"You were so pretty that night," he said quietly, his eyes suddenly sober. "Almost as pretty as you are tonight."

Sarah's own smile, following in the wake of his, ebbed away, and her pulse shifted gears, faintly but undeniably. She'd had her share of compliments, but none had left her quite so speechless, quite so unprepared, quite so . . . pleased.

"Is that outfit new?" he asked, obviously remembering

the packages he'd helped her carry in. He took a step toward her and stood so close he could have reached out and touched her. And she, him.

She swallowed and nodded. "The skirt is," she said in a voice so soft it was barely audible. She was all too conscious of Cade's nearness.

"It's pretty." His voice, too, had grown low and gravelly.

"And the sandals," she added, her eyes welded to his. "They were on sale."

He didn't bother to look at the objects under discussion, but kept his eyes riveted to hers. "They're pretty, too."

"Thank you."

"You're welcome."

The seconds passed. His eyes probed. Her heart thumped against her ribs.

The moment became unreal.

The moment became unmanageable.

But then the moment ended, as unexpectantly as it had begun.

"C'mon, let's eat," Cade said suddenly. "I'm starved." Once more it was the old, comfortable Cade who stood before her.

Sarah blinked, then blinked again. As she sat down at the table, her heartbeat still not regulated, she told herself she was obviously out of practice in receiving simple compliments.

The stars did, indeed, shine through the skylight, though the living room's gold lamplight somewhat diminished their silver glimmer. Sarah sat in an oversized chair, her feet curled to her side beneath the soft folds of her skirt. She cupped a steaming mug of coffee, and on a side table sat the crumbly remains of a brownie.

Cade slouched on the sofa, his feet, brandishing a tiny hole in the toe of one sock, propped up on the coffee table. His broken wrist lay, with increasing restlessness, on a throw pillow he'd dragged onto his lap. He had hardly touched his coffee and hadn't touched his brownie at all. Though he'd professed to be starved, Sarah thought he'd done little more than pick at his food throughout dinner.

"Your wrist's hurting, isn't it?" Her voice shattered the peaceful silence.

Cade looked over at her, carefully adjusting his arm to a more comfortable position and flexing his exposed fingertips. He fought back a grimace as he said, "A little bit."

"Why don't you go to bed?" she suggested.

"It's not that bad," he answered with a wan smile.

"I don't mind."

"I do. We have to turn out the lamp and see those stars we ordered."

"We can see them another night. Go on to bed."

"Later," he said firmly.

He shifted, bringing the coffee mug to his lips. The room was quiet except for a timepiece that suddenly announced nine o'clock in a series of muted chimes. After delivering its timely message, the clock abandoned the room once more to hushed silence.

Sarah sighed; she was end-of-the-day tired but strangely content.

"You haven't mentioned David." Cade's low voice stole through the stillness. "Is that because you're over him or because you aren't?"

At his words, Sarah raised her head. The look on his face, the emotion in his eyes, was difficult to read, but she thought he waited with extraordinary interest for her answer. She explained his concern by reminding herself that he was David's brother; he was a man interested in all things that involved David Sterling. But just how truthful could she be with him? Completely truthful, she decided.

"I was over David long before the divorce," she admitted, her eyes meeting Cade's directly. "I was over David before I even filed for the divorce."

Cade made no response, though the muscles around his mouth relaxed subtly.

Setting down her mug, Sarah sighed, unfolded her legs, and rose, suddenly feeling the need to move. She stepped to the thick oak mantel over the summer-still fireplace and absently fingered the frame of a photograph of the Sterling family—David and Cade, both teenagers; Emma and Jack Sterling, neither of whom she'd ever met. Both had died years before and within two months of each other, Emma of a long, lingering illness, Jack in a car accident. She'd seen this photograph before. David's copy of it had sat in their living room.

Truthful, Sarah thought, her finger tracing the ornate silver frame. She had just told herself she could be completely truthful with Cade. But could she really? Could she say what she really wanted to say? Could she tell him what deep in her heart she'd always wanted to tell him?

"David was seeing other women," she said quietly without turning around.

A silence, as loud as Sarah had ever heard, followed. She instantly regretted what she'd said. Good God, the two men were brothers! What did she expect Cade to say?

"I know," came the quiet male voice.

Sarah's finger stopped its nervous rambling. Her mind stopped its self-flagellation. She turned, her eyes binding with his in gentle bondage. "You know?"

"Yes," he said, studying her closely as if trying to gauge her hurt and absorb as much of it as he could.

Suddenly she laughed hollowly. "Did everybody know? Was I the proverbial last to find out?"

Cade shook his head. "David was . . . discreet."

Sarah tunneled her fingers through her hair. "Well, I guess I can be grateful for that, huh?" A traitorous thought slithered through her mind, then coiled. She knew the question would be better left buried beneath a layer of self-preservation, and yet something all too human forced her to ask it anyway. "The night I lost the baby . . . was David . . ." She swallowed. "Was David with another woman?"

Cade watched her several long moments. Finally, he released a heavy sigh. "Don't, Sarah. It doesn't really matter now, does it?"

He'd given her her answer. He'd found a way to walk that thin line between being her friend and remaining loyal to his brother. She shook her head and smiled dolefully.

"No, it doesn't really matter."

Cade slid his feet from the coffee table and sat up straight, his eyes never leaving hers. "Sarah, it wasn't your fault. It wasn't your failure. It was David's. His infidelities had nothing to do with any inadequacy on your part."

"No?" she asked in a sudden need for assurance that surprised her. She hadn't realized until this very moment how much she needed to hear it wasn't her failing as a woman that had caused her husband to stray. Her mind had accepted the fact that David had problems, but her heart had silently taunted her with the accusation that if she'd been more of a woman, she could have cured his problems, could have kept him in her bed and out of others.

"No," he answered the vulnerable woman now gazing at him with a quiet though desperate intensity. "Definitely not. David has trouble with commitments, especially commitments with women. He always has. When he married you, I thought maybe he'd settle down. God knows, he did love you . . . as much as he's capable of." Cade's voice lowered to a rich huskiness. "Sarah, you're all any man could . . ." The words trailed off, silken wisps of sound left floating in silence. "It wasn't your fault. Don't ever think it was."

She smiled faintly and slipped her hands into the deep slits of her skirt pockets. "Thank you for saying that," she said. "I needed to hear it."

"So how are you adjusting to single life?" he asked after a few seconds.

She shrugged. "Fine, I guess."

"Are you . . . are you seeing anyone?"

"No. I've dated a few times, but . . ." She shrugged again.

"But what?"

"I don't know. None of the guys seemed worth the trouble. Nothing seemed right. You know what I mean?"

His eyes, shaded by golden-brown lashes, darkened almost imperceptibly. "Yeah. I know what you mean."

"What about you?" she asked. "Are you still breaking hearts right and left?" For the life of her she couldn't have explained why she was waiting so intently for his answer.

He smiled slightly. "Yeah. Right and left."

It wasn't the answer she wanted to hear, and she couldn't explain that either.

She was still pondering her response when Cade stretched to turn out the lamp. "Now, about those stars we ordered," he said, his hand never making it to the switch. Instead, he stopped, grimaced, and muttered a sharp "Damn!"

"Cade?" She instinctively took a step toward him.

"It's all right," he answered around a low hiss as he gingerly eased his injured arm back onto the pillow.

"Sure it is," she tossed out. "That's why you just turned as white as a sheet." She took another step toward him. "Go to bed. I mean it." Suddenly a thought crossed her mind, and she frowned. "When did you break your wrist?"

A smile, the same sheepish smile she'd seen earlier in the evening, kicked up the corners of his mouth. "Yesterday," he answered.

"Yesterday?" she repeated in disbelief.

"Early yesterday morning," he qualified as if that made all the difference in the world. "Actually, it was very, very late the night before," he continued when she failed to look appeased.

"And you went in there and cooked and God only knows what else today? You're crazy, Cade Sterling! Certifiably crazy!"

"Right now you won't get much of an argument on that score."

She held out her hand. "C'mon." He hesitated. "C'mon, Cade. Don't be stubborn." Finally, he placed his uninjured hand in hers. She pulled and he stood. "See you in the morning," she said emphatically.

"Sarah, I—"

"Go . . . to . . . bed!" she ordered, nudging him toward the bedroom. She then started gathering up mugs and plates. "I'll clean up the kitchen and be right behind you. To be honest, I'm glad to be calling it an early night. I'm bushed."

Still Cade hesitated, but apparently common sense won out. "See you in the morning," he acquiesced finally.

"Right," she answered, moving off toward the kitchen.

"Hey, Sunshine," he called out softly.

She turned.

"Thanks for coming. You're saving my backside."

A warm smile made its way to her lips. "What are friends for?"

Cade's eyes filled with a fragile, indecipherable emotion. "Yeah," he answered. "What are friends for?" He then turned and walked from the room.

Sarah finished in the kitchen, unpacked the clothes that most needed to be hung, and tumbled tiredly into bed. The new sheets were as lulling as pattering rain on a spring night, and she fell asleep instantly.

Sometime after midnight she awoke with the suddenness of one whose consciousness has been pierced by an indefinable noise. She listened. Nothing. She sat up, pushing the hair from her eyes. Still nothing. Maybe Cade had gone to the bathroom. She sighed and crawled from the bed. Maybe she should go to the bathroom now that she was awake. Minutes later, she stepped back into the bedroom, but instead of slipping under the warms covers again she reached for her cotton robe. She'd just go get a drink of water.

The house was dark, and she relied on her memory and roaming hands to carry her from bedroom to living room. She had just started to grope for the light switch, which she thought she remembered as being on the wall at the juncture of living room and hall, when she heard another sound. Ragged breathing, then a moan.

Her hand found the switch and flipped it on. Light, harsh and glaring after the inky blackness of seconds before, slashed across the room. Sarah's eyes immediately went to the sofa and to the figure sitting there. Cade, barefoot and barechested, wearing only the tennis shorts she'd first seen him in, sat on the sofa, his injured arm cradled in his left and held protectively against his chest. Beads of sweat dewed on his forehead, and the eyes he turned to her were dulled with pain. He tried to smile, but gave up the effort.

"It hurts, Sunshine," he said weakly, his tone tearing at her heart. "It hurts like hell."

CHAPTER THREE

"CADE."

The single word fell from her lips in such an urgent way that, had it possessed medicinal properties, it would have instantly healed all pain, Cade decided.

"I didn't mean to wake you," he apologized, shifting position and paying the price the movement exacted.

"It doesn't matter," she answered. Crossing the room quickly, she came to her knees before him. Her thin robe billowed out around her, leaving her even thinner nightgown in full view. She didn't seem to notice. He did. His eyes swept to the delicate pastel embroidery adorning the gown's bodice, then lowered to move over the shapely rise of breasts the white fabric boldly outlined. Dark shadows proclaimed areolae and budlike nipples. Even with the enormity of the pain engulfing him, he found himself responding in a way typical to a man who's practiced a lengthy celibacy. He cursed his timing. He cursed her gown. He cursed the knife-like stabbing in his wrist. He just cursed.

"Damn!"

"Have you taken anything?"

He shook his head, leaned it back against the sofa, and closed his eyes.

"Surely the doctor gave you something?" she prodded, frustration, disbelief, and a smidgen of panic evident in her voice.

"A prescription," he breathed.

"Where?" She started rising from the floor even as she spoke.

"On the dresser . . . in my bedroom." He opened his eyes and again tried to smile. This time he did, a rueful smile of self-accusation. "But I didn't get it filled."

She stopped in midmotion. "You what?"

"I didn't think I'd need it." A sheepish look once more claimed his face. "Guess I overdid it today, huh?"

Sarah looked at him, then threw back her head to stare at the ceiling. She took a deep breath.

"Sterling," she said at last, "if your wrist weren't already broken, I'd break it myself. How stupid!" she railed before he could utter anything in his defense. "How idiotic! How . . . how . . . Are you certain you didn't fall on your head as well?"

"It's not my head that's hurting."

"Nothing that vacuous would," she threw back.

"Why do I have the feeling you're knocking my intelligence? Aren't you the slightest bit impressed with my courage?"

"I'd be more impressed with a pain pill," she said, whirling and walking from the room.

"John Wayne never took a pain pill for a broken wrist," he volleyed. "And neither would Charles Bronson or Dirty Harry."

From somewhere in the back of the house, he heard, "And they wouldn't fall out of bed either."

"Low blow, Braden. Truthful, but—" The thought died at her reappearance. "Where are you going?"

"Ta gat dis felled," she said around the slip of paper clenched between her teeth. As she spoke, she stuffed her shirt into a pair of wrinkled jeans and bent to tie her sneaker laces. That accomplished, she stood and whipped the prescription from her mouth. "Gilmer does have an all-night drugstore, doesn't it?"

"Yes, but—"

"Where?"

Cade mentioned a street, adding, "You can't go out alone."

"Why not?"

"It's after one o'clock."

"I don't turn into a pumpkin."

"You could get mugged, robbed, raped, murdered—"

"I could also get pain pills."

"Sarah . . ." His voice had turned serious.

"I'm going," she said just as seriously, her staunch expression easing into a smile. "Let me do this for you."

He raised his hand in objection, realizing too late the folly of his action. He grabbed his forearm just short of the cast and bared his teeth just short of a groan.

"Be careful," he relented as he sank back into the sofa's depths.

"Be back in a minute."

A minute and twenty later, Sarah opened the front door and moved at a clipped pace into the living room. Unfamiliar streets and a gregarious pharmacist made her feel as if she'd been gone for hours. She immediately noticed that in her absence the overhead light had been exchanged for the mellower glow of a lamp. She also noticed that Cade was not sitting where she'd left him. In fact, she saw him nowhere.

She had opened her mouth to call his name when she saw toes peeping like tiny sentinels from the arm of the couch. Stepping forward, she peered over the sofa's back. His eyes closed tightly as if to shut out pain, Cade lay stretched out in what looked like an uncomfortable pose, his tall, brawny figure ill fitting the confining measurements of the sofa.

"Cade?" She spoke quietly. When his eyes inched open, she added, "How do you feel?"

He gave a wan smile. "Lousy."

"That good, huh?"

"That good. Look, doll," he added in his best Edward G. Robinson imitation, to which the word *lousy* also applied, "did you make the dope connection?"

She nodded and held the sack aloft. "I'll get you some water."

When she came back into the room, Cade sat up and reached—rather eagerly, she thought, for a man protesting medication—for the glass of water.

"Here you go," she said, uncapping the bottle and tilting it toward her palm. When she held two capsules out to him, his problem became evident. With one hand in a cast, and temporarily immobilized by pain, the other wrapped around a glass, he had no way of taking the pills.

"Would you?" he asked, opening his mouth.

She didn't hesitate. It was only when his moist breath fanned against her skin and her fingers raked gently against his parted lips that she realized the intimacy of what she was doing. And it felt just that: intimate, without a trace of clinical detachment. She told herself she was tired and simply experiencing the surreal effects of still being awake at almost two in the morning.

After he gulped down the pills, she took the empty glass and set it beside the lamp. "Want me to turn back your bed?" she asked.

"I think I'll sleep here," he answered, already preparing to lie down again. "I don't think that bed and I can go another round. I've wrestled it until we're both exhausted."

"Wait!" she said as he started to lower his head back into the pillows. "Let me at least fluff those."

She did, but as she started to pull away, the fingers of his left hand manacled her wrist. Her eyes shot to his.

"Stay with me until I fall asleep. I know it isn't your job description," he added as if purposely trying to lighten the sudden seriousness in his voice, "but, what the hell, I'm the boss. Humor me."

With his fingers still warmly curled around her wrist, it seemed important to her to maintain the teasing mood. "Is this job harassment already?"

But the teasing seemed destined to end, swallowed up by his pain. It wasn't a time for pretense or emotional masquerades. "Stay." Blue eyes met gray in an honest plea. "Please."

She nodded, he released her hand, and she sat down on the solid wood coffee table. "I'll stay only if you'll close your eyes and try to sleep," she said, knowing full well she was lying. He'd asked her to stay, and she would, regardless of the conditions.

He seemed willing, however, to comply with her terms. Lids instantly shuttered his eyes, and for long moments he lay still. She thought he had gone to sleep, and perhaps he had dozed, for he suddenly jerked as if coming back to an abrupt wakefulness.

"Sarah?" he mumbled, his hand searching for hers.

"I'm here," she assured him, clasping his fingers in hers. When she did, he brought their joined hands to rest on the sofa by his side. Sarah felt the crisp cotton of his tennis shorts graze her knuckles.

"Sarah?" he murmured again.

"Hmm?"

"I feel fuzzy."

She smiled. "You're supposed to, idiot. How's the wrist?"

"What wrist?" he asked with a weak grin.

Sarah laughed.

As if irresistibly drawn by the sound, Cade opened his eyes a sliver. "You're the prettiest nurse . . . I've ever had," he muttered, obviously trying to speak around a thickened tongue.

"And just how many nurses have you had, Sterling?"

"Tonsils . . . when I was ten . . . short and fat."

"Thanks. I'm flattered," she teased.

His eyes again flickered shut, and he swallowed, moistening his dry lips with his tongue. He shifted his position, then didn't move for a long while.

"Sar . . . ah." The word was barely coherent and spoken so quietly it was more vibration than sound.

"Uh-huh?"

She waited, but he didn't respond. He was asleep. Dead to the conscious world. Dreaming.

"Sarah," he mumbled from that secret dreamland. "My Sarah."

My Sarah.

It was a simple phrase, uttered in the oblivion of a medicated sleep, yet what it did to the rhythm of her heart was far from simple. In an instant of clarity she knew that belonging to Cade, being cherished by him, would be wonderful. For any woman. Especially for one who'd be gone through a marriage in which she'd felt uncherished. Surely her tumbling heart rate was merely due to a fleeting vision of filling the void in her life that David Sterling never had. But why had Cade referred to her in such a possessive way? The answer must be that he cared deeply for her . . . as family.

And yet, the hand entwined with hers didn't have a familial feel. Even in sleep, it clung to hers, a sweet braiding, a jealous interlacing. Glancing down at their hands, hers so small compared to his, she told herself that she could release their bond. She told herself she *should* release it. But she didn't. Couldn't or wouldn't. Instead, her thumb slid the length of his index finger, discovering the feel of skin she knew yet didn't know.

He sighed as if in reaction to her exploring touch, and at the sound Sarah's gaze shifted upward, stopping at the chest expanding in a sleep-even rhythm. As she watched his chest rise and fall, she thought back to the image she'd had while listening to him shower. Her question concerning hair was answered. It did, indeed, mat his chest, but not as heavily as his brother's did. Whereas David's hair was dark brown and densely forested his chest, Cade's was golden-brown and sprigged his body more gracefully. A swell of curls dusted his upper pectorals, thinned at midchest, then flared again at his trim stomach. And a narrow line did trail lower and lower—just as her eyes were doing. Her gaze followed the line to his navel, then rested on the elastic waistband of his white shorts—she told herself she shouldn't be doing this—before brazenly sliding farther down. A sense of impropriety, coupled with a warm tingling, washed over her. Guiltily, she redirected her gaze.

To his lips. They were parted now, emitting slow, steady breaths. The warm tingling she'd hoped to rid herself of flared even hotter, and her mind raced back to that Sunday

afternoon when he'd kissed her. His lips had been unde-
manding, understanding, the lips of a friend giving comfort.
But now, sitting here, the woman in her wondered what
those lips would kiss like in passion. Would they devour
completely? Would they share sweetly? Would they murmur
words to spin the head and inflame the senses? She felt her
own senses reeling under the onslaught of flash-fire feelings.
She also heard a moan. She thought it was his, but then
realized it might have been her own.

She yanked her hand from his as if she'd suddenly touched
a white-hot poker. He stirred, rolling his head and flexing
his knee, and finally settled back into a deep slumber. What
was happening to her? she thought, confused and appalled
by her reaction. This was Cade, for heaven's sake! Her
friend! Her brother-in-law! Good God—this time she was
certain she groaned—she'd die if Cade ever found out about
her shameless fantasies.

She went to bed vowing he never would.

The morning sun speared its way through the skylight in
Sarah's bedroom, awakening her to the new day and re-
charging her spirits to their usual sunny summit. Yesterday,
she told herself, could be easily explained. Well, maybe not
easily, but it *could* be explained. She'd been under a lot of
strain, both from the divorce and the launching of her new
career. She'd also been without a man for a long time.
Obviously too long, she added, remembering the way she
had responded to Cade. But it had nothing to do with Cade
personally, she hastily clarified. Nothing whatsoever. And
she was going to stop these forays into madness and get on
with the job she'd come here to do.

This she promised herself as she dressed in navy slacks
and headed from the bedroom to the kitchen. On the way
she stopped in the living room to turn off the lamp that had
burned all night. She deliberately avoided looking at Cade,
who was asleep on the sofa. Why test the strength of her
new resolve so early in the morning? And before coffee?

Within minutes, a mug of the steaming brew in hand,
she quietly opened the front door and gathered in the morn-

ing paper. She was a little surprised to see it was the *Dallas Morning News*. Her surprise waned when she realized that Cade had probably made special arrangements so he could keep up with his comic strip. Tucking the newspaper under her arm, she made her way toward what she assumed to be the studio. Her assumption proved correct.

This room, too, was designed with a skylight. Square and crystal-clear, it encompassed nearly a third of the ceiling. The studio also boasted a row of narrow clerestory windows, obviously there for light rather than view. The room's view was Rigby Rat and his paramour, Ms. Mona. The comic strip characters peeked from every nook and cranny—from the cork bulletin board, from the tilted drawing table, from the tall-legged stool, from the pleasantly cluttered desk, and again from the filing cabinet. On the circular back wall was a mural, a serene scene of whispering stream and tree-silhouetted sky. Rigby Rat basked on a sun-dappled lily pad while Ms. Mona peered, or perhaps leered, at him from parted green ferns. Sarah smiled and sat down. Not even bothering with the headlines, she flipped open the paper to the comics section and read.

Ms. Mona, her long, thick, mascaraed eyelashes fluttering provocatively, her enormous lips—once described as carnal red—puckered in an exaggerated kiss, was caught in the act of swinging a lasso in Rigby Rat's direction. The small, wiry rodent, no match for Ms. Mona's large, buxom physique, was forced to rely on the only weapon he had: his dry, sarcastic wit. Turning to the reader just as the rope encircled his neck, he said, deadpan, "I love subtlety."

As always, the strip made Sarah laugh. She was giggling still when a movement at the doorway arrested her attention. She glanced up sharply. And into Cade's sleepy eyes.

His bare shoulder leaning against the doorjamb, he looked as though he'd just crawled off the sofa, though the mug in his hand indicated he'd made a stop on his way to the studio. His hair needed combing off his forehead, and his cheeks and chin begged to be relieved of a stubbly growth of beard. The white tennis shorts, wrinkled and riding low on his hips, looked as though he'd slept in them, which, indeed, he had. By every standard of good grooming, he should have looked awful. Which only proved, Sarah thought, that you couldn't rely a whole lot on the standards of good grooming.

"Hi," she said, telling herself that the subtle racing of her heart was due to the fact that he'd startled her.

"Good morning," he returned with a lazy smile. "I see you found my office."

With a gesture that encompassed the room and its comic strip memorabilia, she said, "How could I miss it?"

His mouth eased into an indulgent grin. "It is a bit over-done, isn't it? But I'm always sketching, and fans just keep sending me mementos I can't throw out. Actually, I kind of like it. I call the style early Rigby baroque."

Sarah's mouth twitched at the corners. "I like it, too," she said before adding seriously, "How are you feeling?"

"Like cotton has been ginned in my mouth and like a herd of revenge-crazed buffalo have tap-danced across my body."

Sarah's smile instantly reappeared. "I think the medi-cation is responsible for the first. The sofa is probably the second culprit."

"You don't think a herd of buffalo tap-danced across my body?"

"Probably not. No hoof marks." She took a sip of her coffee. "How's the wrist?"

"Pretty good," he answered, looking down at the cast contrasted against his bronze stomach. "In fact, it seems to be the least painful part of my anatomy right now."

"That's a good sign," she said, wondering how he man-aged to stay so tan draped over a drawing table so much of the time.

"I'm hoping it's a good sign," he responded. Then he nodded at the newspaper. "What's RR up to today?" At the surprised look on her face, he explained, "I never know the order in which they're going to run."

"Oh, I never thought of that. Anyway, today Rigby loves subtlety."

Cade smiled, nodded, and brought the mug to his lips.

"How did you get the *Dallas Morning News* delivered to your doorstep?"

"I have an arrangement with a neighbor. For six months, he picks it up at a convenience store and drops it off; then I reciprocate the other six months."

"Not a bad plan," Sarah said approvingly.

"We small-town boys are smart."

"Tell me," she said, "is Ms. Mona ever going to catch Rigby Rat?" Three months earlier *Time* magazine had called that very question one of the most pressing issues of the decade.

Cade shrugged. "Who knows? Sometimes the most unlikely couples fall in love."

The room suddenly grew quiet, creating a serious tenor totally inappropriate for the flippant question she'd just asked. Sarah sensed the mood change, but was unable to explain it. Any more than she could explain the intensity in the blue eyes watching her or the strange, quivery feeling that intensity left her with.

"Well," Cade said, pushing from the door and shattering the confusing moment, "let me go shower and shave, and we'll get to work." He turned but took only a few steps before turning back. "Thanks for last night ... the pills ... and for staying with me."

Sarah shrugged in a dismissive gesture. "No problem. You'd have done the same for me, wouldn't you?"

His eyes darkened; then he turned and disappeared from the doorway.

Only later did Sarah realize that he'd never verbalized an answer. But then, he hadn't needed to. She'd seen it in his eyes and known it in her heart.

"Are you sure I can do this?" Sarah asked skeptically some thirty minutes later as she sat at the desk in a coiled pose that could only be called ready-to-run-at-the-first-chance.

"I'm certain you can," Cade assured her. "You're an artist, remember? Just don't panic." As if to underscore the point, he slid with a casual litheness onto the tall stool, hooking his feet on the bottom rung and veeing his jean-clad legs in a very male fashion.

Sarah diverted her eyes from the provocatively strained denim and back to the crowded desk before her. "That's easy for you to say. I don't even know what half this stuff is." She stared helplessly at Cade's hodgepodge of unlabeled bottles and tubes and jars, so unlike her own highly organized work supplies.

"Like what?"

"Like everything," she countered in wild exaggeration.

"You know what most of this is," he said, rummaging through the supplies. "This is masking tape, this a Pink Pearl eraser, this a ruler—incidentally, used in cartooning only to measure with, never, never, to draw with—these are pencils with soft lead, these are charcoal pencils, these are Globe bowl-pointed pens, these are felt-tip pens—"

"What's this?" Sarah asked, holding up an unmarked jar of a white substance.

"Bleedproof opaque white. Takes out errors. Make good friends with it. It's invaluable."

"So you do think I'm going to be awful?" she asked, her eyes wide with concern.

"I think that if you make fewer mistakes than I do, I'm going to be real unhappy. I buy this by the case."

"So errors are permitted?" Sarah asked, suspiciously eyeing another unlabeled container.

"Permitted and expected," Cade answered, grinning devilishly and indicating the object of her interest. "That's rubber cement; I'm sure you're acquainted with the stuff. It's also for errors."

Sarah gave a sarcastic sigh. "If you're trying to ease my mind about this project, Sterling, you're using the wrong approach."

He stretched across her and snatched up the rubber cement, leaving in his wake a spicy scent of after shave. His grin appeared once more as he applied the viscous substance to a sheet of paper. "It also has one other useful function. It's good to play with when nothing's going right."

"Keep that handy," she ordered, by sheer will ignoring

the after shave taunting her nose.

"My working method is pretty simple," Cade proceeded. "Everything is roughed out first on bond paper, cleaned up on tracing paper, and next transferred onto two-ply Strathmore via a light box." He tapped what Sarah did recognize as a light box for tracing. "From there, you'll ink the final copy. Each strip always starts with a thumbnail sketch, then the lettering of dialogue, then filling in the pics with gestures and expressions. Borders are done freehand with a thick felt marker. You got it?"

What Sarah got was another whiff of after shave, and this one refused to be so easily ignored. It wafted about her nose, smelling fresh and potent and male. It jabbed unmercifully at her unguarded feminine senses and brutally slaughtered her resolve to forget Cade as a man.

"Got any questions?"

"One," she said, slightly breathless. "What am I doing here?"

He laughed, disregarding the panic in her voice, which only partially had to do with the job facing her.

Within the hour, however, her world seemed to right itself. Caught up in a project she found truly fascinating and artistically challenging, she shoved her disturbing feelings to the background. Only once did they threaten to escape their bonds, and that was when Cade vacated the stool and pulled it up to the drawing board for her. The leather still held the warmth from his body, and when she seated herself and soaked up that warmth with her own body, she experienced a sensual awareness, subtle and fleeting but powerful enough to play havoc with her steady breathing. She quickly berated herself for the reaction and purposefully lost herself in Cade's current plans for the strip.

And concrete plans he had.

"I'm going to break Rigby Rat's forefoot . . ."

"You're going to do what?"

"I'm going to put him in a cast." Cade held up his own plastered limb. "If it's good enough for me, it's good enough for ol' Rigby."

"You're a sadist," she accused.

"Ah, but Ms. Mona's going to thank me," Cade added with a smile. "Rigby can't run as fast now."

Sarah had to agree it was a clever idea, especially when she had sketched the panel in its entirety. The first segment showed a warlike rugby match among swamp creatures, the second segment showcased Rigby Rat in a cast, trying to explain to a macho hippo, who wore gold chains about his neck and was constantly trying to get Spanish moss to grow in lieu of hair on his bare chest, just how the break had come about. With the hippo sniggering aspersions on Rigby's athletic ability and masculinity, Rigby Rat turned to the reader in the last and final segment and delivered the line: "At least I didn't break it falling out of bed."

The first sketch made, Sarah set about cleaning it up on tracing paper. At Cade's instruction, she enlarged and whittled, shifted and erased. Her mood fluctuated between the panic Cade told her to avoid and the swift thrill of elation when she got something right. At all times, Cade encouraged, making an obvious effort to put her at what ease he could. Also obvious was his own impatience at being an onlooker in a project normally all his. More than once, in the throes of enthusiasm, he reached for a pencil with his right hand, only to be painfully reminded of his incapacitation.

After one such powerful reminder, he barked out, "No, no, make that fuller! Make the rugby match look like a fracas of flying fists and feet."

"Like this?" she asked, ignoring a tone she knew was aimed solely at his frustrating disability.

"Even more," he instructed, leaning forward from his position behind her and taking her right hand in his left to crudely guide it into a series of charcoal lines. "Good . . . good . . ." he praised, releasing her hand to its own creative powers, though he neither removed his hand from the table nor stepped away from her. She continued to draw, sketching dust clouds and arms and legs at weird angles. "That's it! Great, Sunshine!"

"Is it really all right?" she asked, excitement beginning to bubble in her veins because she felt it was, indeed, right.

Right at last. She quickly swiveled toward him, eagerly seeking his opinion. "Do you . . . like it?" The last two words stumbled from her lips in a whisper, their sound stolen by the male body trapping her against the edge of the drawing board.

A thousand sensations stormed her in one cataclysmic second. The hair on his arm ticklishly abrading her forearm. His leg solidly pressed against her knee. His shoulders sheltering her in their masculine width. That devastating after shave making yet another raid on her common sense. And his eyes . . . eyes burning a scorching blue as they studied her with an expression mirroring her own startled look. Slowly, those eyes lowered from hers and dropped to her mouth.

He was going to kiss her! she thought wildly.

Her lips tingled. Her breath grew shallow. Her heart pounded.

And then the phone rang.

CHAPTER FOUR

SARAH JUMPED, RAMMING her spine against the drawing board, while Cade's head jerked toward the sudden blaring noise.

Seconds swirled by. The phone rang again. In one swift motion, as if nothing of any consequence had just happened, Cade snapped to life, walked the few feet to the desk, and grabbed the receiver in the middle of the third ring.

"Hello?"

Cade had moved to answer the phone with all the normality of a man not caught up in a moment of insanity, Sarah realized, chastising herself for her ridiculous notion that he had been about to kiss her. Dear God, now she was projecting her erotic fantasies onto him!

"Cade?" the phone's male voice queried.

"David!" Cade spun toward Sarah, his eyes locking instantly with hers. A muscle jumped near the corner of his mouth, and his jaw suddenly tautened.

Two thoughts scrambled through Sarah's mind: One, knowing that David was on the phone was subtly upsetting to her; two, knowing that David was on the phone was likewise upsetting to Cade. Just as she was wondering why, the tension chiseled on Cade's face miraculously disappeared.

"Hey," Cade said, his tone now warm and brotherly, "how are you?"

"Look, I'm not calling at a bad time, am I? I mean, you sounded a little strange."

"No, no," Cade answered, deliberately turning away from Sarah. "Now's fine. Whatcha up to?"

"Forget about me, Little Brother. What's this rumor I hear?"

"And what rumor is that?" Cade teased, knowing what was coming next.

"I hear you're laid up with a broken wrist."

"Wrong. I'm not laid up."

"But you do have a broken wrist?"

"That's what the doctor says."

"Hell, Cade," he drawled, "why did you go and do that?" Without waiting for an answer to his rhetorical question, he added, "How'd you do it?"

Cade told him.

A loud whoop of laughter shot through the line. "I'm sorry," David said, trying to control his laughter. "I'm really sorry." Another round of uncontrolled guffaws broke out. "For godsake, are you serious?"

"Would I lie about something like that?" Cade responded, grinning.

"Well, tell me one thing. Was she worth it?" He next made a comment that at best was sexually crude.

Cade's grin faded. "I was alone at the time." He knew it was probably hard for David to understand that some men did sleep alone, at least sometimes. Though he'd had his own share of women, Cade had never understood his brother's insatiable appetite. However, he'd tried not to be judgmental. He'd succeeded, at least partially, until Sarah.

"Alone?" There was an incredulous inflection in the one word, followed by the all-knowing, "Oh, I get it. You're protecting the lady's reputation."

"Alone, as in all by myself," Cade countered.

"Sure," David added smugly.

Cade gave a small smile, somewhere between amusement and sadness.

"Look, kid," David said, quickly segueing to another topic, "I thought I'd run up tomorrow and see for myself that you're all right."

Cade felt his heartbeat erupt into a series of dots and dashes that signaled a red alert. "No! I mean, I'm fine. It's only a broken wrist. There's no need for you—"

"I've got business in the area anyway," David explained. "I'll pick you up, and we'll have a bite of lunch."

"Lunch?"

"Yeah, maybe that barbecue place down on . . ."

Cade didn't hear the rest of the sentence. All he heard was his name whispered from across the room. Swiveling, his eyes found Sarah's.

"Go on to lunch," she mouthed, nodding toward the phone.

"To be honest"—David's voice tugged once more at Cade's attention—"I'd . . . I'd like to talk to you." The words were delivered in a tone Cade didn't associate with his brother. It bordered on a plea and instantly appealed to the deep feelings he had for the man at the other end of the line. Despite his younger years, Cade had always felt responsible for his older brother in a way that defied logic yet made perfect sense to the heart. There were times, especially in the past months, when Cade had cursed his sense of responsibility and loyalty.

That sense of responsibility and loyalty now forced him to ask, "Is something wrong?"

"No, no," David countered immediately. "Just wanted to talk to you about something." His mood lightened, almost purposely it seemed. "What if I pick you up about noon?"

Cade hesitated, trapped beneath a ton of conflicting emotions represented by the voice on the phone and the presence of the woman mere feet away. "Noon's fine," he said at last.

"Hey, Cade?" David asked as if a thought had just occured to him.

"Yeah?"

"Which arm?"

"Right, of course."

A descriptive expletive followed. "What are you going to do about the strip?"

Cade's heart dove into his stomach. "I . . . uh . . ." His eyes flashed briefly to Sarah, then slid guiltily away. "I'll have to hire an artist."

"That's a king-sized pain in the— Damn, there's my buzzer. Gotta go. I'll see you tomorrow at noon." The phone went dead in Cade's hand. For long moments he didn't recradle it; he simply listened to the dull, flat dial tone that seemed to echo the dull thudding of his cowardly heart.

At last, stretching forward, he eased the receiver into its cradle and turned slowly to meet the eyes he knew would be watching him.

"That was David," he announced unnecessarily. Looking as though he didn't know what to do with himself, he stuffed the fingers of his good hand into the back pocket of his jeans. "He wants to take me to lunch tomorrow."

"Fine . . . that's fine. Getting out will do you good." Sarah laid the cartoon sketch, the one she suddenly realized she was still holding in nerveless fingers, back onto the slanted board. "I . . . I need to get some art supplies. I'll just plan to go around noon tomorrow." She didn't add it, but both knew she meant to be gone when David arrived and to stay gone until David left. She knew it was what Cade obviously preferred. And Cade knew she knew.

He also knew she was surprised—he could see it in her eyes, hear it in the strain of her voice—by his omission. Omission, hell! He had out-and-out lied to David about having to hire an artist! His stomach knotted into a thousand endless spirals, and he felt the need to get off by himself. To be alone so he could try to sort through what had just happened.

"Let's call it quits for the day," he said abruptly. He circled the desk, walked with crisp strides from the room, then, with the slamming of the kitchen door at his back, fled into the Thursday morning sunshine.

Cade felt the hot rays of the sun lacerate the thin knit of his shirt; he felt the pearls of sweat form on his back and run in salty rivulets down the length of his spine. The burning Texas sun, sometimes so purifying, today felt punitive. Cade fancifully told himself it was retribution for what he'd just done.

Why had he lied to David? he wondered, moving off toward the meadow and the tranquil silence it offered. Why hadn't he admitted Sarah was working with him? He'd planned to tell David; in fact, he'd reasoned that there was no way to keep the news from him—at least not for long. And why shouldn't he tell him? It was an innocent arrangement, a work agreement. Yet, at the moment of truth, he had denied Sarah's presence. Why?

Cade stopped his aimless meandering as if waiting for the answer to catch up with him. Reaching down, he snapped up a thin-stemmed weed, brought it to his mouth, and chewed it in absent contemplation. Far in the distance, a herd of white-faced Herefords grazed in pastoral serenity, and the sound of peaceful lowing—a mockery of his own turbulent feelings—reached his ears. Monarch butterflies waved in whisperlike flutters as they dined on the honeyed nectar of orange milkweed, while the scarlet trumpets of standing cypress and the white of fleabane dotted meadow and field.

He sighed wearily. The answer was quite simple really; it was admitting the answer that was difficult. He hadn't wanted David to know that Sarah was there because he had wanted her to himself, if only in this small way. He didn't want to share her.

Cade pulled the bitter-tasting weed from between his teeth and threw it to the ground. And this work arrangement was far from innocent, at least as far as he was concerned. Hell, he'd almost kissed her just moments before the phone rang! That admission brought a fresh pang of guilt.

Guilt.

Good Lord, he thought, had any man ever known more about that specter? He knew its every gradation, its every shade, every tint, every hue. He knew the niggling guilt present even in moments of joy and happiness. He knew the braver guilt that made unexpected skirmishes during those unguarded times when he unwittingly allowed himself the luxury of a few moments' peace of mind. And he knew the bold, brazen, brute guilt that hunted in the raven night, in those haunted hours when he cursed himself for loving the wrong woman.

No. Sarah wasn't the wrong woman. He knew that with a heart's certainty, with a soul's sureness. And he was fault-less, blameless. He hadn't asked to love his brother's wife. Dammit, hadn't he prayed a thousand times that he didn't? And yet his love persisted. Just as his guilt persisted.

Persisted and grew and sometimes threatened to stifle him. Because he could never forget that he'd fallen in love with Sarah while she was still wearing his brother's ring.

But she was no longer wearing that ring. There were no longer wedding vows to respect. There was no longer a need for this guilt.

Cade imagined the sun now cleansing him with warm rays of absolution. It gave him the strength to renew his resolution. Tomorrow he'd tell David that Sarah was work-ing for him.

And sometime in the future he might be able to tell David of his love for Sarah. Surely David would understand. Surely David would forgive. Surely David would sanction. Surely . . .

The image of an angry ten-year-old David flashed through Cade's mind. Fists clenched, David was red-faced, thin-lipped, and ready to do battle for a basketball he hadn't played with in months. All because Cade wanted to use something stamped with David's ownership.

Cade glanced up to see a gray-ruffled cloud spilling across the sun. He wasn't surprised. He'd felt the grayness some-where in his soul.

Staring out the narrow window, Sarah watched Cade disappear into the sprawling, sun-splashed meadow. He was upset; she sensed it. Why hadn't he told David she was working for him? She had waited, dreading David's reac-tion, but Cade had deliberately kept the knowledge from him. She didn't understand, any more than she understood the strange sense of deliverance she'd experienced at Cade's decision. Any more than she understood her heartfelt relief at hearing that a woman hadn't been sharing Cade's bed when he'd broken his wrist. Any more than she understood her sense of loss at realizing that he hadn't been about to kiss her.

She pulled in a long breath and expelled it on a sigh. What was happening to her? Ever since Cade had opened the door yesterday, her world had teetered on an uneven axis. The familiar had become unfamiliar, the normal, abnormal, while comfortable had given way to a condition only degrees away from unbearable. Feelings and sensations stormed about as wildly as long-penned stallions. What she wanted more than anything in the world was to discuss these aberrant feelings with her best friend, but that she couldn't do. *Cade* was her best friend.

Just as a gray-tinged cloud wandered across the bright morning sun, Sarah reeled in her frustration, turned from the window, and walked from the studio. Maybe a cup of hot coffee would restore her sanity. Even as she moved toward the kitchen, she realized she was pinning a lot of hope on simple caffeine.

The studio grew silent and still, except for the gentle rush of chilled air breathing from the overhead vent. The zephyr ghosted downward, sending the leaves of the ivy plant on the desk into delicate vibration and fluttering the comics page of the Dallas Morning News. *A rustling sound, a whispered sibilation. A sound of sprinkling fairy dust and magic. Lines shimmered and blurred and sparked to life.*

Rigby Rat stepped from the page and, with an impatient shudder, shook loose the lasso encircling his furry neck. With a scudding shuffle, he scurried across the desk, scaled the side of Sarah's forgotten coffee mug, and swung to sit on the rim. Bright black eyes took in the sights around him, which in large measure was Ms. Mona, dressed in ostentatious black satin and sequins, slinking à la Mae West over ruler and masking tape. She perched on a jar of opaque white. There was sadness in her wide, thick-lashed eyes.

"He lied," she sighed.

"She wanted him to," Rigby Rat countered knowingly, consolingly.

"He was going to kiss her."

"She wanted him to."

"He loves her."

"She wants him to," Rigby Rat said, adding, "but she doesn't know yet that she does."

"He's hurting," Ms. Mona said, blinking back a seldom-seen muskrat tear with a sweep of her broomlike lashes.

"It's an old hurt."

"She's beginning to hurt."

"All old must once be new."

Ms. Mona sighed again, this time heaving her balloonlike bosom well past her chin. "Being human is no picnic."

Her companion was about to agree when he saw Ms. Mona's eyes brighten to their usual Vegas-at-night glow. With a sprinting movement, she jumped from the jar and grabbed up the Pink Pearl eraser, which stood exactly three-quarters of her muskrat height.

"What are you doing?" he asked suspiciously.

"I'm going to erase their past," she said, proud of her wise solution. "The past is the problem."

"No, no, you mustn't!" Rigby Rat cried with such haste and concern that he almost toppled headfirst into the mug's muddy pool of coffee. "Without the pain of the past, human beings can have no joy of the present."

"Oh," she said, surprised at learning this bit of human lore. "Being human really isn't a picnic, is it?" Her shoulders slumped in defeat, she breathed another sigh that sent a pencil rolling end over somersault end. Suddenly, her eyes sparked with another idea. "I know," she said, wrestling with the pencil until it stood weaving like an unwilling Maypole. "I'll write them a future."

*The pencil swayed; Ms. Mona grappled. In the
end the pencil won and clunked against the side of
the mug. Rigby Rat instantly shinnied down the pencil's long column. He plopped onto his muskrat fanny,
at the same time sending Ms. Mona to her Mae West
fanny. The pencil thudded to the desk like felled tim-
ber.*

*"In due time," Rigby Rat said from the spot where
he'd landed. "We'll see about a future for them in
due time."*

*The eyes Ms. Mona turned to him were loving.
"Do you mean that?" Without waiting for his answer,
she pursed her lips.* Smack! Smack! Smack! Smooch-
smack!

*"Ah, Mona," Rigby Rat chastised as he wiped at
the scarlet lipstick tattooing his face. There was a
don't-do-that quality to his voice, but an overriding
gleam shone in his beady muskrat eyes.*

The day passed.

After a dinner Sarah prepared and she and Cade ate amid
conversation deliberately bright, she returned to the studio
to work on the cartoon begun that morning. Cade went with
her. Neither spoke of David or the call or the morrow's
ensuing lunch—topics that hung in the air like storm-laden
clouds—but as they worked side by side, the sweet magic
of friendship took over, and strain gave way to companion-
able talk and laughter.

"My Ms. Mona looks like a cross between Dolly Parton,
Miss Piggy, and Greta Garbo," Sarah lamented.

"She does not. She looks just like mine," Cade said in
Sarah's defense. He then added with a devilish smile, "Although Kermit the Frog just called. Said to tell you thanks
for the big bazooms"—with one hand he mimed Dolly
Parton's voluptuousness—"and that he definitely does not
'vant to be alone' tonight."

Sarah grinned and wadded up a discarded sheet of paper.
It hit Cade midchest. Grins turned into laughter. Laughter
fell away to silence, while two pairs of eyes searched each

other with interest.

"Well," Sarah breathed, "I think I'll call it a day."

"Me, too," Cade agreed, standing.

"Good night," she said, rounding the desk and heading for the door.

"Sarah . . ."

She stopped, turned, waited. Questions once more hung in the air.

He sighed. "You did well today. You're a gifted artist."

An hour later, still wide-eyed and restless and ultra-aware of every sound coming from Cade's room, Sarah wished she were, indeed, gifted. Gifted enough to sort through her muddled emotions and arrange them into coherent meaning. Right now, she'd settle for anything that made the slightest sense.

David Sterling stood facing the mantel, his hands buried deep in the pockets of expensive trousers, his attention absorbed in the family photograph. Cade Sterling stood across the room, the thumb of his good hand hooked loosely in the pocket of his jeans. His attention was on his brother.

A thousand memories burst to life in Cade's mind, swamping him in emotion. Memories of only the two of them all these years following their parents' deaths; memories of that first lousy Christmas, when David was twenty-two, Cade seventeen, and both were scared-stiff kids, hurting so badly neither thought he'd survive; memories of David dropping out his junior year of college to make a living while Cade finished his senior year of high school; memories of David never finishing college but hounding, hounding until his little brother did. Memories of laughing together and wishing they could cry together despite the fact that men cried only in the solitude of the night. Memories of fighting together but always managing to care about each other in the fighting. Memories of serving as David's best man at his wedding . . .

"I still miss them," David said, turning and interrupting what had become a painful thought for Cade. Cade's attention instantly shifted, and he struggled to make meaning of his brother's remark. He finally did.

"Yeah," he said, taking in the photograph. "I miss them, too." In the span of time it took to say it, Cade realized he was surprised at David's comment about their parents—surprised not at the missing but at the open admission of it. David had always shied away from displays and confessions of emotion.

Confession.

The word tossed Cade into another arena of thought. He hadn't yet confessed that Sarah was working for him. He tried to do it several times during lunch, even on the drive back to the house, but the words stubbornly refused to come. He told himself the moment hadn't been right. He also told himself his stalling could get him into a passel of trouble, possibly soon. Especially if Sarah got tired of playing this stay-away game he was sure she didn't understand. He looked at his watch and estimated just how likely it was that she'd interrupt them. The late hour made him conclude: very likely.

Damn! he thought. David never came in this way. It was always a quick lunch, with both men going back to work with a "Good to see you" and a "Let's do it again soon." But not today. Today, David had come in at Cade's obligatory invitation. He had come in and wandered about the living room, almost as if he, too, were stalling. Cade wondered if it had something to do with this talk he'd said he wanted to have, a talk that hadn't yet materialized. Cade was curious, even concerned, but mostly he just wanted David to leave. For this selfish sentiment, he cursed himself. He also checked his watch again.

"You want some coffee?" Cade forced himself to ask in the spirit of social civility.

"Yeah. That sounds good," David said, obviously groping for any delaying tactic. Cade sensed his brother's reluctance to leave, but the hands on his watch were moving swiftly. He even toyed with the notion that David already knew about Sarah's working for him and was slyly tormenting him. On the heels of that paranoid idea, he told himself that that was exactly what it was: paranoia at its best—or worst. David knew nothing about Sarah's working

for him, and even if he did, his style was confrontation, not
subtle mental torture.

"You need any help?" David called out in afterthought
to Cade's retreating back.

"Uh-uh," Cade responded, disappearing into the kitchen,
where he set coffee to perking.

This is it, he promised himself as he swiped his moist
hand down a pant leg. He was going to walk back into that
room and tell David that he'd hired Sarah to help him. He
had to. If he didn't, he was putting his own ass in a sling.

"David . . ."

The other man looked up from his place on the sofa. He
had taken off his sports jacket and tie and carelessly tossed
them over the back of the seat.

Cade hesitated, cursed himself for the hesitation, then
sighed. He felt the old posterior being hoisted into a sling.
". . . the coffee will be ready in a minute."

David's reply had nothing to do with coffee and sounded
as if it were the result of an inner pep talk similar to Cade's.
"I have something to tell you." Quick, straightforward, and
to the point.

Cade heard the seriousness in David's tone and, despite
his own problems, reacted with genuine concern. "What is
it?" he asked, taking the chair across the way. "What's
wrong?"

David gestured vaguely, expressing emotional discomfort. "Nothing's wrong. I just wanted you to know something. I mean, I thought it would be better if you knew."

"Knew what?"

David's dark eyes stared resolutely into Cade's blue ones.
"I'm in therapy."

The first thought that crossed Cade's mind was physical
therapy, and he quickly scanned his brother's body. He looked
more than fit.

"I'm seeing a psychologist," David added.

Cade's eyes widened.

David laughed nervously. "Are you that shocked?"

"Uh . . . uh . . ." He returned a half laugh. "Actually, I
am surprised." Why deny the obvious when it must be

smeared all over his face?

"And disappointed?"

Cade's eyes locked with David's, and there was a fierce streak of protectiveness when he spoke. "Disappointed? Hell, no. Why should I be disappointed?"

The other man gave a crooked, self-conscious grin. "I don't know. Maybe you thought I was perfect."

Cade's mouth slid into a curve. "Do I look that stupid?"

David laughed; then his grin disappeared. "No. No, you don't." He leaned forward, dropping his hands and his gaze between his knees. He glanced up. "I have some problems I'm trying to work through. Losing Sarah was a blow," he added.

At the mention of Sarah's name, Cade's heart rattled in his chest.

"She had begged me to get counseling, so I figured better late than never." For long moments, David said nothing else. He spent the time fidgeting and finally sighing. "I can't get over her, Cade. Her memory just won't die. And I've gone through a hell of a lot of women trying to forget her."

At the soft-spoken words, words he never heard his brother speak before, Cade's heart plummeted to his feet. Even at that painful moment, however, he was aware that David had conveniently failed to mention the women he'd gone through while still married to Sarah.

"I know I have a lousy track record with women," David added as if reading his brother's mind, "but if she'd just given me time, I think we could have worked out our problems. I think she was seeing someone at the last, but . . ."

"Why do you say that?" Cade managed to get out.

"Just a feeling. Sometimes when I'd look at her, I could see another man on her mind." His eyes dulled to the cloudy color of torment. "She never said anything to you, did she? I mean, I know you two—"

"No," Cade denied vehemently, "there wasn't anyone else. I mean, she never mentioned anyone to me. I think you're wrong."

David shrugged. "Maybe you're right. Anyway," he added

as he idly reached forward and fingered the sunglasses on the coffee table, "I'm going to try to get myself straightened out. I'm going to try to find out why I'm so damned destructive in my relationships with women."

Cade said nothing. He just sat watching David toy with the sunglasses. Sarah's sunglasses. He silently muttered an expletive.

"The psychologist is using phrases like 'undeveloped self-image' and 'arrested positive psyche.' Whatever the hell all that means."

He picked up the sunglasses.

Cade held his breath.

"Who knows," David said with a forced smile, abandoning the sunglasses back to the table—Cade's sigh of relief was almost audible—"maybe I'll give Sarah a call if this psychologist can work a minor miracle. She loved me once, right?"

Cade swallowed. "Right," he said, his answer little more than a gust of air.

"Look, I'd better run," David said, glancing at his watch. He rose from the sofa, gathered up his coat and tie, and started for the door. "I'll take a raincheck on that coffee."

"Sure," Cade said, following him, astonished that he was performing so normally. "Thanks for lunch."

"Enjoyed it. And I'm sorry about your wrist."

"No problem," he answered, adding truthfully, "I'm glad about the therapy."

"Thanks." He turned but immediately pivoted back. "Did you find someone to help you with the strip?"

There was a slight pause before Cade said, "Yeah. I hired someone."

He rationalized his incomplete answer in every way he could. He was protecting David. Wasn't undergoing therapy a vulnerable time? He was protecting Sarah. Maybe David was serious about straightening out; maybe he wasn't. And hadn't she already done her share of suffering? Even in the midst of his brilliant rationalization, however, he wondered if the one he was really protecting wasn't himself. The thought made him feel like a heel.

Seconds later, he watched as David pulled down the drive, spewing a fine spray of cinnamon-colored dust behind him. In the near distance, Cade saw a navy van. A thin film of sweat dewed his forehead when the van slowed at the turnoff, hesitated, then drove on by. The beads of sweat instantly chilled at his relief. No, he thought, he felt lower than a heel.

Sarah found him in the kitchen. She knew instantly that something was wrong; his shoulders were slumped, and his stare was vacant.

"Hi," she said softly, a little timidly.

He glanced up sharply. "Hi."

"How . . . how was lunch?" She nervously raked back a strand of hair.

Cade didn't answer her question.

Which prompted her to ask another.

"How's David?"

That particular question remained unanswered, too.

"I didn't tell him." Blunt. Terse. Expectant.

She didn't need to ask what he hadn't told David.

"He's getting counseling," Cade continued.

"Counseling?"

"He's seeing a psychologist."

"I see," Sarah said, pleased at the news, though relegating it to a position of lesser importance than what was currently transpiring. Funny, she thought in the far reaches of her consciousness, at one time David's getting help had meant more than anything else to her.

"I thought knowing you were here working for me might only complicate the issue," Cade said.

Sarah nodded her agreement.

It was hardly an adequate explanation for remaining silent. Both knew it, but both accepted it anyway, each wondering why.

Seconds ticked by. Sarah fought the urge to comfort him in his obvious distress, while Cade increased his misery by telling himself he should reveal to Sarah everything David had said. But he didn't, and that, too, mushroomed his misery to unbearable proportions.

"You ready to go to work?" he asked suddenly in a clipped voice. "We need to finish out yesterday's panel and start on today's. You might need to work on..."

He continued to talk, but Sarah tuned out what he was saying and concentrated solely on the way he was saying it. He sounded short, curt, as if he were angry with her. But what had *she* done?

He opened the cabinet, reached for a mug, and started to pour coffee. His left hand wobbled slightly. "The rugby match looks fine, but—damn!" he exclaimed as the coffee pot jiggled, spilling hot coffee on the cabinet and down the front of his jeans.

"Cade!" Sarah cried, snatching up the terry-cloth rag, running it under cold water, and starting to wipe at the dark pool spreading across the snug navy denim. "Cade, are you all right?" she asked, barely aware of what she was doing.

She daubed the cool cloth quickly, down his left thigh and up again before jumping over to the stain covering the front of his jeans. As she swiped the rag back and forth, her fingers brushed first against the snap, then rasped against the metal teeth of a zipper. Her hand followed the length of that zipper, up and down, patting and stroking. Beneath her fingers, beneath her palm, she felt a steamy moistness, felt the outline of brief underwear, felt his stomach muscles tight and firm. Even as she noted the trimness of those muscles, she felt them tauten and constrict. And along with them tightened thigh muscles and...

Sarah's hand stopped. The fullness beneath her touch lay rigid and hard, straining against stretched denim in a way that was unmistakable and probably uncomfortable. Maybe even downright painful. Yanking her hand away, her eyes flew to his, the gray of dismay colliding with the impassioned glow of blue.

"I...I'm...I'm sorry." Her words echoed, seeming to bounce off his heaving chest. "I was only..." She was aware of her own delayed reaction, a warm seeping of feminine feelings that flowed over her body, leaving in its wake a flush, a tingling, a heaviness.

"I'll go change," he said in a voice as thready as hers.

She watched as he walked from the room. Embarrassed, she collapsed against the kitchen counter. It was an instinctive male reaction to touch, she told herself in explanation. It had nothing to do with her. Then why, she wondered, did his heart seem to be stammering at the same speed as hers? And why did she want more than anything in the world for them to be strangers just meeting? Strangers who were free to touch . . . and kiss . . . and ease sudden, exquisite aches. Strangers who were free to love.

CHAPTER FIVE

"YOU'RE AWFULLY QUIET," Cade said a week later from the passenger side of the van. He sat ankle squared to knee with his left arm sprawled across the back of the corduroy-covered seat.

Sarah sliced a look through the early evening darkness, her eyes grazing his briefly before shifting back to follow the path the headlights blazed down the highway. She smiled. "I was just thinking about your rugby buddies. They seemed nice."

"Yeah," Cade agreed, yet with less enthusiasm than he would have felt a couple of hours before. The two men's outrageous flirting with Sarah had irritated him.

When he and Sarah had gone into town late that Friday afternoon to mail off the first week's production of the comic strip, they had planned to have a nice quiet celebration dinner. Their plans had gone awry midmeal with the arrival of Mike Palmer and Joe-Bob Ross. The two Texans had sauntered into the restaurant in cowboy boots and high spirits and had insisted upon dragging up chairs and joining the fun. Ordinarily Cade would have welcomed their company. Tonight he hadn't.

In a town as small as Gilmer, news traveled fast, and the grapevine already whispered that Cade Sterling had a woman staying with him. Mike and Joe-Bob had been perfectly willing to respect their friend's territorial rights until they discovered the nature of the relationship.

"Hey, man, you mean you two are related?" Mike Palmer had asked, surprise scoring his craggy but handsome face just moments before jet-black eyes gleamed with obvious pleasure.

"Kind of," Sarah said, strangely wishing she could deny their family ties completely. She wasn't sure why; the admission just seemed emotionally uncomfortable in terms of the feelings she'd been secretly fighting all week.

"We *were* related," Cade pointed out, hoping his friend picked up on the subtlety of verb tense.

He didn't. "Well, well," Mike drawled, "this does add a new wrinkle." As he spoke he eased his arm around the back of Sarah's chair and leaned into her intimately. "Hey, darlin', you wouldn't want to have an affair, would you?"

"Don't be so crass, Palmer," Joe-Bob interrupted, finishing up the obscenity he had just scrawled on Cade's cast, pushing his friend's arm out of the way, and draping his own arm around Sarah's shoulders. "Of course the lady doesn't want to have an affair with you. She wants to have one with me. Don't you, honey?" Bushy eyebrows crawled in an exaggerated leer above hazel eyes flecked in green.

Sarah laughed at the men's good-natured teasing.

"You two want to can it?" Cade said, not nearly as impressed by their clowning around.

An unwanted-but-couldn't-refuse-politely beer later, as he was settling the bill and Joe-Bob was visiting the men's room, Cade observed Mike making an honest-to-goodness pitch for a date. Cade's stomach had cramped until he saw Sarah, with tact and a kind smile, decline. He had then ushered her out into the night and away from his buddies faster than real courtesy dictated.

"Mike asked you out, didn't he?" Cade said quietly as Sarah turned the van onto the winding dirt road leading to the house.

Once more her eyes coasted to his. Even through the ebony night, she could feel his intense gaze. "Yes," she answered, tacking on after a pause, "I told him no. He's a nice guy, but..."

"But what?" Cade asked when she said nothing more.

One shoulder rose in a shrug. "He's not my type."

"What is your type?"

The seriousness in his voice made her glance at him again. "I really don't know," she answered just as earnestly, trying to decide why no man *had* appealed to her in the span of a year and a half...and why the man she'd once been married to seemed least of all her type.

"Mike owns some of the best pastureland in the state and one of the biggest herds of cattle. He has a good sense of humor, he's a man of integrity, and the ladies obviously like him."

Sarah's laughter danced in the air. "You sound like his agent."

Cade's shrug looked casual but wasn't. "I'm just telling you what you passed up tonight."

"I'm certain Mike's the catch of the year," Sarah said, "but he's still not my type."

Both fell silent, Cade wondering if Sarah sensed his possessive attitude, she wondering if the possessiveness she sensed was based in reality or in this fantasy world she'd insisted on living in since arriving in Gilmer. The truth was, the idea of Cade feeling possessive toward her was a surprisingly pleasant idea, one she didn't dare examine too closely.

She parked the van in front of the house. A hushed stillness surrounded them, signaling journey's end, but neither Sarah nor Cade moved to get out. Tension instantly materialized. Unspoken words mingled with gauzy, unclear thoughts; awareness clashed with awareness.

"Thanks for dinner," Sarah heard herself say to ease the stress of the moment.

"You earned it."

"It has been a rough week," she said, thinking in terms of more than just work.

"Yeah." The one word seemed to underscore her silent thought.

Another round of tension, this one stronger, skipped about the van's interior.

"What did Joe-Bob write on your cast?" she asked as another weapon against the strange feeling closing in on her. It was a feeling of being on the verge of something you could never go back from, the feeling that the week's emotional confusion was building to a flash of understanding.

Cade grinned, which Sarah sensed more than saw.

"You don't want to know."

"When you put it that way, Sterling, I've got to," she said, rising to the challenge and flipping on the overhead light. Both blinked in response.

She took his hand in both of hers and read the wildly scribbled message on the cast. Pink instantly flowered in her cheeks, and she groaned. "You're right. I didn't want to know. The world seems to have a singular opinion as to what you were doing when you broke your wrist." Her unplanned remark referred to David's comment of the week before.

"People can't resist the razzing," he said. Long moments passed before he once more spoke, this time in a voice softer than stardust at twilight. "I wasn't with a woman."

He wanted to say that he hadn't been with a woman since he'd kissed her a year and a half ago; she wanted to ask when was the last time he had been with a woman. Crazily, she didn't want to think of him as ever having made love. Contrarily, she wondered what kind of lover he was.

Their eyes were locked in the delivery of mute messages when, suddenly, she realized she was still holding his hand. When his fingers brushed against hers, a tingling started, and the touch of the plaster cast was inexplicably erotic. He glanced down at their hands, then back up at her. Sensations, hot and sensual, shot along the nerve fibers of both bodies. Jerking her hands away, Sarah switched off the interior light, thankful for the swift, consuming darkness.

As if by mutual agreement, they unlatched their doors, climbed from the van, and started for the house. Cade unlocked the front door and shoved the key into a pocket.

Instead of going in, however, he turned, his eyes finding hers.

"Let's take a walk. I want to show you something." With a gentle pressure at the small of her back, he guided her toward the meadow. Sunbaked grass crunched beneath their feet, and stickseed weeds clung greedily at the legs of their jeans.

The something he wanted to show her was an obsidian sky chock-full of the rarest of treasures: shimmering diamonds dripping in sprinkled delight before a perfect moonsphere of liquid silver. Silver and night. A combination as old as the world, as new as the next rotation of the earth. It was a summer sky filled with star-dancers, a summer night in which lovers' hearts were filled with star-dreams.

"Aren't they beautiful?" he asked softly. "Those stars are the reason for the skylights. I wanted them to pour into the house every night. Look up there," he said, pointing. Sarah's gaze followed the muscular outline of his outstretched arm. "That's Ursa Major . . ."

"The Big Dipper," she said, automatically adopting the same tone of reverence she heard in his voice.

"Uh-huh. And that's Ursa Minor, the Little Dipper . . . and there's Draco, the Dragon . . . Cygnus, the Swan . . . and way up there"—he indicated a spot farther north—"that's Cassiopeia. And way, way up there . . ."

As blasphemous to his enthusiasm as it was, Sarah's attention shifted from sky to man. In dark silhouette, he stood with shoulders somehow broader than she'd remembered. His profile was a sculptor's exquisite creation: a furrowed forehead carelessly, irresistibly frothed with hair, a nose, strong and straight; cheeks, firm; and a chin wide and jutting with strength. Her eyes lowered, roaming over chest and waist before dipping to the leanness of hips and thighs.

The memory of the kitchen scene a week before rushed at her, leaving her with the same warm wave of weakness now as then. Neither had spoken of his blatant male response—not even when he'd returned minutes later with dry jeans and a fanatical need to work—yet the subject seemed always crouched just below the surface of forced normalcy. A brittle tentativeness hung in the air, a squall on the verge of crashing to shore. Though she didn't understand it, she accepted the growing disquiet between them. And curiously waited. For what, she wasn't certain.

"Sarah."

As the sweet song he made of her name floated to her, she raised her eyes. Cade stood before her, night shadow, consummate male. His after shave blended with her perfume, and both scents melded with the fragrance of wild honeysuckle and tame magnolia. In the distance a languorous breeze flitted among the leaves of the old oak tree. The same breeze fluttered a wisp of Sarah's hair and, as it did so, the wind seemed to sigh that the wait was almost over.

"Your hair is like the night," Cade whispered as if he fought against saying the words but fought with a strength too frail. He was equally helpless not to brush the errant strand of hair from the corner of her mouth. Once done, his thumb lingered, rough pad to soft lip. "And your eyes are the color of starlight."

"You can't see my eyes," she said logically as her heart began to pound.

"Wrong." The palm of his hand settled on the side of her face, where it burned despite its satin caress. "I can never *not* see them."

The two stared through the southern night, each seeking the other's eyes illuminated in the moon's phantom glow. Slowly, with the speed of a thousand eternities, Cade's head angled and lowered.

"No," Sarah whispered, knowing his intention, knowing she must stop him, yet knowing she really didn't want to.

"Why?" The word blew against her lips like a fair zephyr.

"Because . . . you're my brother-in-law."

He shook his head. "No," he breathed, "I'm your ex—brother-in-law."

As his head closed the distance, she knew in a flash of clarity that this moment was what she'd been waiting for.

She'd been waiting for it for a week, a year and a half, a lifetime.

His lips fused with hers in a gentle bonding. She made no effort to return the kiss but passively allowed his mouth to know hers with warmth and pressure and unbelievable tenderness. After sweet, brief seconds, he lifted his head, though his face still hovered above hers. Then they stood quietly, gauging each other's reaction.

No inadequate words spoiled the moment, only a recognition of feelings—hearts beating far too fast, breathing shallow and rapid, slight tremors shaking bodies and souls and familiar thoughts about kinship.

Then, with a moan of long denial and depleted restraint, his mouth took hers again, this time passionately, demandingly. Helpless, she responded to his urgent command. His mouth slanting over hers, he forced her lips to part and followed her willing surrender with the invasion of his tongue. It buried itself in her receptive moistness as if this were the sanctuary it had so long sought. Sarah's pulse thudded erratically, and she swayed against him. The hand at her cheek slipped to the back of her neck, while his cast anchored at her waist. Her hands glided over his ribs and slid around his back. The kiss deepened, his tongue dampening, dueling, drawing every response she could give.

It had been so long since a man had kissed her, she thought, wanting him closer, ever closer . . . so long . . . and never like this . . . never. The kiss of moments before she could rationalize as similar to the innocent one they'd shared so many months ago, but this kiss, this honeyed persuasion of her senses, was plainly, simply a kiss between a man and a woman. Man and woman. Sarah and Cade . . . Cade . . . Cade . . .

"Cade!" she cried, wrestling from him at the brutal realization of just whose arms she was in, just whose lips were kissing her in such divine ecstasy. Stumbling, she stepped back, her chest heaving in passion and confusion.

He took a half step toward her. "Sarah?" His voice, too, sounded of passion but also of the savage beast named fear.

"No! Please." With that plea, she started for the house, first at a walk, then at a run. She heard him call her name again, this time in desperation, but she didn't stop. Fleeing to her room, she closed the door and, with her heart still pounding and her lips still stinging, buried her face in her hands.

Dear God, she thought, what had she just done?

"We have to talk," Cade said exactly forty-four seconds later as he threw wide the bedroom door.

Sarah whirled, her startled eyes colliding with his.

He opened his mouth, closed it without saying a word, raked his hand through his hair, and opened his mouth again. This time words tumbled out, though at their best they were incoherent. "I didn't mean . . . I mean, I did mean . . . The kiss was . . . You should have stopped me if . . ." He halted, hung his head, and stared blankly at the floor. "I don't know what to say," he said, at last raising his eyes to hers. He gave a self-mocking laugh. "I've played this moment out a hundred times in my mind, and now that it's here, I don't know what to say. Great, Sterling!" He shoved his fingers back through his hair. "Just great!"

Some part of Sarah's brain processed the fact that this moment had had such importance to him that he'd planned for it, but she could only marginally consider it. She was too caught up in what had just happened and the fact that Cade was more upset than she'd ever seen him. Even in the midst of her hazy thoughts and churning emotions, she longed to comfort him.

"Oh, Sarah," he sighed in exasperation, "there are so many questions I want to ask. So many questions I have to have answers to."

"Like what?" she whispered because her voice refused to be any stronger.

"Have I just ruined a good friendship?" The prospect plainly devastated him. "Have I shocked you? Dammit, was I wrong about your response a minute ago?"

To this last question, she wanted to give a defensive lie, but she couldn't. She owed him the truth. Maybe she even owed it to herself. Shaking her head, she answered, "No.

No, you weren't wrong." She eased to sit on the side of the bed, wedging her trembling hands in a prayerlike pose in her lap. The feel of his lips on hers, the feel of her lips begging more of his, was more than a memory; it was still a burning reality. "Oh, Cade," she whispered, looking up at him with beseeching eyes, "what's happening to me? To us?"

Crossing the room, he squatted down before her. "What do you think is happening?" he asked gently, the question hovering between dread and hope.

"I don't know," she answered, negating her response with the stricken, "Oh, God, you're my broth—"

"No!" He silenced her with a sharp denial. "I am *not* your brother-in-law. And even when I was, we weren't related—not in any blood sense." He forced himself to take a calming breath. He also forced himself to say the one thing that he knew he must. "I'm attracted to you, Sarah. Physically, emotionally. In all the ways a man is attracted to a woman."

The words spun in her ears, making her uncertain she was hearing correctly. And yet, what he was saying made sense. The tangible, building tension that had loomed between them all week, the way he had just kissed her, his male reaction to her when she'd wiped at the spilled coffee—it all made sense. It also made her heart throb with a wild excitement.

"I didn't mean it to happen, Sunshine," he added. "God knows I didn't. It just did."

Shifting his weight, he rose, one knee creaking in protest, and moved to stand at the foot of the bed. His back was to her, but she had the feeling his soul was very much before her.

"I don't even know when it began," he said, shoving his fingers into a back pocket. "The first time I realized it . . . the first time I let myself realize it was when you were in the hospital. When I kissed you, I—" He halted as if the memory were so powerfully overwhelming that it robbed him of speech. Finally he continued. "When you told me you were asking for a divorce, I had to get away from Dallas,

had to give you and David time to work out your problems
if you could. I prayed you would; I prayed you wouldn't.
Mostly, I just prayed the thought of you wouldn't drive me
totally insane."

"You never called. I mean, after the divorce." It was a
curious thing to say, she realized, almost a gentle reprimand.

"No," he said without hesitation, throwing a look back
at her. "I wanted to give you time to get your life in order.
The truth is, I guess I was just scared. I had no idea whether
you'd ever thought of me in terms of ... anything other than
family. When I broke my wrist, I told myself it was a
legitimate excuse to see you, to see if I'd purged you from
my system." A small laugh shook his broad shoulders. "So
much for purging you."

It all fell into place, Sarah thought. Cade's moving to
Gilmer without so much as a hint of warning. Nothing more
than his single note wishing her luck with her new business.
His discomfort when David had called the week before. His
omission that she was working for him. Yes, everything fell
into place ... except for her own feelings. And yet, weren't
they falling, like jagged pieces of a puzzle she'd been too
cowardly to work, into place, too?

"Sometimes in the night," she said, speaking to herself,
to him, and so softly that he had to strain to hear, "I'd lie
in bed thinking of that Sunday afternoon in the hospital. I
felt so alone ... until you came. So lost ... until you held
me. I told myself you only kissed me to console me, to
comfort me, but ...." She trailed off, watching her fingers
thread themselves together.

He had turned slowly. "But what?"

Raising her head, she heard herself say, "I ... I wanted
it to be more than that. It had been for me."

The words purchased her freedom, freedom to finally
admit to herself an attraction that she'd first tried to deny,
then tried to rationalize and excuse, then tried to closet away
entirely. Suddenly her feelings blazed with a crystal bril-
liance, though they left her dazed, with emotions staggering
for balance.

"What are you saying?" he asked, retracing his steps and once more squatting before her. He studied her with blue eyes that were very dark, very wide, waiting. When she said nothing, he prompted, "I need to hear you say it."

In answer, she stretched out a hand, started to trail her finger across his cheek, then hesitated. The hesitation lasted only a second. Her finger touched his cheek tentatively, experimentally, in a pattern of discovery. It was as if she were seeing him for the first time.

"I've been having these wild fantasies of you," she said more bluntly than she could ever have imagined herself doing. "I thought I was going crazy."

"If you're going crazy with fantasies," he said, "I am, too." He paused, then whispered, "Say it, Sunshine. Say the words. Say you're attracted to me. Woman to man."

"I'm attracted to you," she said softly, adding in a hushed tone, "woman to man."

His hand covered hers, flattening her palm to his cheek. He closed his eyes, inhaled, and sighed deeply. Both simply savored the wonder of the moment.

But the moment was fraught also with bewilderment, uncertainty.

"Cade, what are we going to do?"

His eyes slowly opened to meet hers. He swallowed hard. "What do you want to do?"

She shook her head. "I don't know. This is so new to me. I mean, you and me . . ."

She pulled her hand from his, rose, and stepped around him. He let her move away, gave her the space she needed. He, too, came to his feet, but he stood where he was, watching her, wanting to comfort her but not allowing himself to.

"I feel . . . I don't know, that this is somehow improper," she admitted.

"It isn't."

"I know, but some people might think it is."

"What if they do?"

She ignored his response, her eyes skewering him for an

answer to another question. "And what about David? Even though you're my ex–brother-in-law, you're not David's ex-brother."

A look of pain raced across Cade's face, clouding his eyes. "Do you think I haven't thought of that? Believe me, guilt and I are old friends."

"David won't understand," she said.

"Forget David. What do *you* want?"

She hesitated. "I don't know," she said, answering him as truthfully as she could. "Can you understand that?"

He watched the emotions warring on her face, sighed, and replied, "Yes."

"Things are happening so fast," she tried to explain, in the end giving up and throwing both hands in the air. "Maybe you should find someone else to help you with the strip."

"Is that what you want?" Pain punctuated the question. "To come this far and go no farther?"

She considered. Did she want to go no farther? Did she want to walk away from Cade now? Never to kiss him again as she had in the meadow? Slowly, she shook her head. "No."

"Neither do I," he said, coming to stand a mere foot from her. She thought he was going to touch her, but he didn't. Except with eyes blue and begging. "Give us a chance, Sarah. I won't push, I promise. Just give me a chance to make you lo—need me as much as I need you."

Need. How could he make her need him any more than she did right this moment? She needed his arms, his understanding, his friendship. She needed all that was he. "I'll stay," she whispered.

Relief flooded his face, and his eyes lowered from hers to her lips, where they remained until two hearts beat wildly. But he didn't kiss her. Instead, he deliberately stepped away from her in what looked, even to her, like a forced effort. "I have some work I need to do," he said. "And you need some time to think."

She nodded, silently thanking him for his sensitivity. "Good night," she said.

"Good night."

He was already halfway across the room when she called out, "Cade?"

He turned. Waited. And thought she was the most beautiful woman he'd ever seen.

"We'll always be friends, won't we? I couldn't bear it if—"

"Always, Sunshine," he interrupted. "You can take that to the bank."

Eleven fifty-three. Sarah thrashed about for the thousandth time, and for the thousandth time her nightgown chokingly twisted beneath her. In utter frustration, she tossed back the covers and threw her legs over the side of the bed. Sleep was a commodity she couldn't have purchased with all the money in the world—not with the thoughts stampeding through her mind. Thoughts. Feelings. What *was* she feeling?

She smiled, raking back tousled hair. She was feeling exactly the way she had felt on her first date: scared and excited. But she was no longer fifteen, and Cade wasn't the callow Brian Gilbert. And the relationship Cade was suggesting was not the uncomplicated one of two young kids trying to grow up. This relationship had the potential to hurt. David and Cade were close, and she'd never forgive herself if she came between the two brothers. And she knew in her heart that there were some, maybe even her friends and family, who'd view the relationship as inappropriate.

Fluffing the pillow with excessive jabs, she lay back down and stared through the skylight at the stars flickering their astral ballet. They reminded her of Cade. And his kiss. And his warm, male voice telling her he needed her. And his begging her to stay, to give them a chance. Her fingers eased to her lips, lips indelibly etched with the taste of his. As curling tendrils of desire slowly uncoiled, she realized her staying had never really been in question. She'd never really had a choice.

Cade sat in a chair on the inner circular patio, staring up at the millions of blinking stars. They reminded him of

Sarah. But then everything good in life reminded him of Sarah. Dear God, his feelings were finally out in the open, and she hadn't run. In fact, miracle of miracles, she'd confessed an attraction to him. He'd wanted to tell her he loved her, but he knew that was taking her too far too fast. She was confused by an admission she'd obviously tried hard to keep to herself. She needed time to readjust her thinking about him, needed time to see him as a man. He'd promised her that time, and he'd give it to her. They both needed it. She, to accept him in this new light, he to figure out how to deal with David. David. If he were really still in love with Sarah . . . Damn! Why was nothing ever simple? The usual guilt threatened to slice at his happiness, but Cade thwarted it. Not tonight, he reasoned, rising, pushing back the glass door, and entering the house. Tonight he'd think no further than Sarah . . . and the fact that she'd remembered that long-ago kiss, too.

> On the deserted patio, a fountain gurgled in the silence. The gurgle gave way to a splash as the water in the tiny pool billowed upward from the force of a furry muskrat head. Rigby Rat, beads of moisture pearling his face, gave Ms. Mona a thumbs-up, all-is-progressing-as-we-planned sign.
>
> After adjusting the straps of her minuscule pink-and-white polka-dot bikini, she returned the sign, then stretched out on a palm leaf to soak up a star-tan.
>
> "What's guilt?" she asked, smearing herself with the gel of a nearby aloe vera plant.
>
> "A painful human emotion," he replied, his glossy brown coat gleaming in the moonlight as he backstroked across the pool.
>
> "Like falling on your backside?"
>
> "Exactly. It's the feeling a human being gets when he falls flat on the backside of his conscience."

For all of the following day, Cade strove to pick up the comfortable threads of their friendship, and he made the supreme effort not to touch Sarah in any way. He seemed determined to give her time. That night, however, she went to bed restless and feeling a near palpable strain. She slept fitfully and dreamed of the hospital kiss. This time it was blistering with passion—as was her response.

The next morning found them at the kitchen table, each engrossed in a section of the Sunday paper. Coffee mugs sent clouds of steam upward, while a nut-topped coffee cake tempted with smells of spice and forbidden calories.

Sarah folded her section of the paper and reached for another just as Cade completed a similar action. Their hands brushed. Days before, dominated by feelings she couldn't understand, she would have pulled quickly away, but now she sat watching, mesmerized, as his hand folded gently about hers. Her hand seemed lost in his but safe and protected. It was a feeling warmer than the August sun plunging through the skylight. Her eyes moved to his, sleepy blue and smiling. With motions slow and deliberate, he drew her hand to his mouth and kissed first her palm, then her tiny-veined wrist. The intimacy of the kiss left her breathless . . . and wanting more. But it was a more that was forced to defer to his promise of time.

Four days later, on a Thursday morning shouting life, Sarah and Cade were in the studio putting the finishing strokes to another cartoon panel.

"What do you think?" she asked.

"Good," he said, coming up behind her where she sat on the stool and peering over her shoulder. "But put some polka dots on Ms. Mona's bikini."

"Polka dots?" Sarah questioned with a grin, which he immediately returned.

"Yeah, I think she'd go for polka dots."

"Polka dots it is."

The tiny circles drawn, Sarah swiveled toward him. "How about . . ." Her voice trailed off when she found herself imprisoned between the massiveness of his chest and the edge of the tilted drawing board. It was a repeat of a similar scene.

Neither spoke, though their eyes sparked with hunger.

They had not touched, not even so much as hand to hand, since Sunday morning. Sarah knew he was giving her time. Sometimes she thought he was giving her too much.

"Were you going to kiss me that morning?" she asked, her voice slightly breathless.

Cade knew exactly what morning she was referring to. He grinned—they had done a lot of that the past few days. "Did you want me to?"

She grinned back. "That's a question, not an answer. Were you?"

"Did you think I was?"

"That's still a question. Were you?"

"Maybe," he said, taking the cartoon out of her hand and laying it on the table behind her.

"That's an evasive answer," she said, now truly breathless.

He stepped closer, thigh to thigh. His head lowered. "I was . . . and I am. What do you call that?"

"About time," she whispered seconds before his mouth possessed hers.

That night they played chess. Or attempted to. Mostly their eyes just looked and lingered and probed. Hands grazed and found ridiculous reasons to touch.

Absently Cade maneuvered his knight into a pitifully vulnerable position. He glanced up.

"Your move," he whispered. Both knew his words had nothing to do with the game.

Her hand on an inappropriate pawn, her eyes welded to his, she moistened dry lips with the tip of her tongue. Cade's ragged breath tumbled from his chest.

Second after second crept by on feet of indecision.

"Are you going to play that thing . . . or kiss me?" The very words sent two sets of senses reeling.

Leaning across the card table, her mouth brushed his, brushed again, then settled firmly. His lips parted beneath hers, and his breath, still uneven, rushed forward in a sensual hiss. His hand slid to the column of her throat, his thumb resting where her pulse hammered. She sighed; he sighed;

the pawn clanked onto the board. Taking the reins, Cade's mouth opened wider, curving over hers intimately, moistly. His tongue teased her lips, at last tunneling into the sweet, sweet haven she offered.

He felt desire stalking him with satiny stealth.

She felt desire ribboning her in velvet bondage.

Ultimately, reluctantly, he pulled from her but rested his lips only a breath away. His eyes were still closed.

"Do you have any idea what you do to me?" he whispered.

"Yes," she whispered back, knowing exactly because he was doing the same thing to her. And the crazy thing was, it seemed right. Right as in born to be kissed by him.

CHAPTER SIX

WHY HAD SHE never before noticed how sexy his legs were?

Two days after the chess game, from her seat at the table, Sarah pondered this question as she watched Cade roam about the kitchen. Potatoes were baking, thick steaks were laid out, ready to broil, and he was at the moment wrestling with a fresh green salad. Dinner was running late because they'd opted to work that Saturday and had quit only an hour before to shower and dress.

The reason she had never noticed his sexy legs, she decided, sipping a gin and tonic, was that, although she'd certainly seen him in shorts before, she'd never seen him in a pair that exposed quite so much.

The pale yellow shorts revealed long, exercise-taut legs dusted with a forest of golden-brown hair from thighs all the way down to ankles. The shorts sported a discreet, inverted V cut on each thigh, allowing a peek at tanned skin, a tempting peek that intrigued Sarah. Why was that tender skin as golden as the rest of his leg? Did he sunbathe in the buff? That thought intrigued her far more. As did the thought that his underwear must be briefer than brief, since not even a hint of it showed. Then again, maybe he hadn't put on any at all following his shower. That possibility totally destroyed the uniform cadence of her breathing.

"Sarah?" His delivery indicated he had called her name more than once.

She guiltily jerked her head up from his shorts.

"Could you help me with this?" he asked, indicating his cast and a stubborn head of lettuce.

"Sure!" she said quickly. As she stood, straightening the leg she had tucked beneath her, she tugged at her own navy shorts, as if by doing so she could lower Cade's to a level that wouldn't play havoc with her senses. The action was wasted motion.

"Where's the salad bowl?" she asked, glad of the diversion and already tearing the lettuce into chunky bites.

Cade shoved a wooden bowl in her direction and awkwardly busied himself chopping scallions.

"How would you like to go to Dallas next week?" he asked. Glancing up, he added quickly, "Actually, you don't have a choice. I have to go, and I obviously can't drive."

She mirrored the grin he wore. "When you put it that way, Sterling, I'd love to go. Do I get to ask why?"

The scallion he was trying to cut with one hand rolled away from the knife and tumbled from butcher block to floor. A mild oath and a rinsing later, Cade pushed the green onion toward Sarah. "You want to do this?" he said, immediately tailgating the question with, "A toy company has approached me about manufacturing a stuffed Rigby Rat."

Sarah glanced up, a smile curving her lips. "Oh, Cade, that's wonderful."

He returned her smile. "Yeah, I'm pleased." His grin broadened. "Hell, I'm ecstatic."

"You should be."

"Of course," he added practically, "it may come to nothing. I need to meet with company representatives and discuss the particulars. See if we can come to some sort of deal."

"Will they do Ms. Mona, too?" Sarah asked. "They can't do Rigby without Ms. Mona. It's sexist. Besides, fans won't stand for it."

"Hey, I may use both those arguments," he said, his thonged sandals slapping as he walked to the refrigerator and removed the rest of the salad makings and a can of beer.

The vegetables—radishes, celery, carrots, and plump red tomatoes—he piled near Sarah, while he popped the top from the can of beer. Leaning back against the counter with one leg crossed over the other at the ankle, he swigged a long, serious swallow. From over the top of the can, his eyes wandered to Sarah's legs. Damn, but they were sexy! Long, willowy, and kissed by the sun to a bronze color that begged to be caressed. He wondered when she found time to sunbathe. He wondered *where* she sunbathed. The tan looked as if it covered every inch of her body. Surely she didn't sunbathe nu—

"What?" He glanced up sharply when he realized she'd spoken.

"I said, 'What day are we going?'"

"Probably Wednesday or Thursday," he answered, allowing himself one more look at her legs and thrusting the idea of her nude to the back of his mind. "I thought you could see some of your clients while you're back."

"That'll work out fine," she said as she methodically chopped, diced, and sliced. "I've got several layouts ready for final approval." For the next few minutes they discussed her business and Cade's hopes for the toy deal. The salad finished, she reached for a terry towel and was in the midst of wiping her hands when she looked over at a lounging Cade. She frowned. "Hey, just a minute. Isn't this *your* night to cook?"

"I am cooking," he replied, smothering a grin behind another sip of beer.

"You are? It looks remarkably as if *I* am," she parried, indicating the bowl nearly spilling over from her endeavors.

The grin, one that would have stopped the heart of any woman at fifty paces, refused to stay hidden. "You noticed that, huh?"

"I noticed," she said, trying to sound stern around the echo of his smile.

"Can I help it if you're easily persuaded?" he said as he set the beer can on the counter and stepped across the room to the steaks. He bent to slip them under the broiler. "Can I help it if you're a soft touch for a sob story? Can I—Hey!" he bellowed as the tip of the terry towel connected with his derriere.

Sarah smirked. "Can I help it if you bent over?"

The face Cade turned to her was a wild paradox. His eyes laughed just inches above a mouth purposely forced into a grim line. "You're going to pay for that, Ms. Braden," he said, grabbing at the terry cloth, the other end of which she still held, and reeling her toward him by slowly wrapping the cloth around and around his good hand. The solution to Sarah's problem was simple: Turn loose her end. But it wasn't nearly as much fun as hanging on.

"Don't, Cade," she pleaded, her smile growing bigger the closer she got to him. "I'm sorry," she lied.

"No, you're not."

When he finished reeling her in, he yanked the towel from her grasp and, slipping his arm around her waist, hauled her to him.

"Truly, I—" she started, only to have the words chopped off when his body snuggled against hers. His legs, bare below the yellow shorts, seemed intolerably sensual as they tangled with hers. His skin felt warm—hot—and the wisps of hair chafed her thighs in a way just short of maddening.

"You're going to have to take your punishment, babe," he said in the worst Bogart imitation she'd ever heard.

"And what punishment is that?" she breathed against a mouth that loomed potently near.

"The most torturous kind," he whispered seconds before his mouth closed over hers.

He tasted of beer, but it was his mastery of kissing— the nip of her bottom lip between playful teeth, the exquisite skimming of her top lip as he tongue-stroked—that intoxicated her senses. He felt so good. His kiss felt so good. His knowing her with this kind of intimacy felt good. And right. And somehow ordained.

"You call that torturous?" she sighed when his mouth left hers.

"It damned sure is for me," he said, the kind of torture

he was enduring very obvious. Sarah felt his tormented body steel-hard between them. Days before, this closeness would have shocked her. But no longer. Now it simply excited her. Instinctively, she even stepped nearer. "God, those shorts are driving me crazy," he groaned as he slid the flat of his hand onto her hip to press her more fully into him.

"Yours are driving me crazy, too."

"Mine?"

"Yes."

"Good, we can share a room at the asylum."

This time his lips savored hers with a slow, fevered urgency, which she welcomed and returned in kind. His tongue taunted her with promise and then fulfilled that promise by sinking deeply into her warm, pliant mouth. She surrendered. She conquered. She yielded to spiraling sensations so powerful they left her body weak.

"I think . . . I think the steaks are burning," Sarah whispered against his lips, which at that moment were kissing one corner of her mouth. He strayed to the other corner, where his tongue prodded and teased.

"What steaks?" he whispered, his lips once more rolling greedily, insatiably, onto hers.

The meal passed in a blur of burned steaks, chilled Chablis, and looks of open longing. After washing the dishes, they settled side by side on the sofa, feet propped on the coffee table, to watch TV. They saw a horror movie, and at the climax of screams and loud music, Sarah automatically gripped Cade's bare thigh. Minutes later, when she turned to him to comment on the movie's plot, she found his eyes on her, eyes hot with thinly veiled desire. Her gaze lowered from his to her hand. She started to pull it away.

"No," he had said, his hand smothering hers. "Leave it. If it feels good to you."

The hand stayed, but the movie was never quite the same. Suspense had given way to the feel of warm skin; murder and mayhem, to firm muscle; terror, to the delicious tickling of downy hair. And though her heart still pulsated at a shuddering pace, the reason for that erratic beat was vastly altered. It now had nothing to do with the movie and everything to do with the man beside her.

Twenty minutes later, Cade clicked off the TV by remote control, but neither he nor Sarah made any move to get up from the sofa. Sarah's hand, now in her lap, tingled; Cade's leg, suffering from withdrawal, tingled as well. Their eyes grazed again, this time braving a longer look. Cade spoke. Honestly.

"It's getting harder and harder to say good night to you."

"I know," she replied as truthfully.

He sighed deeply, following it with a sly grin. "So why don't we postpone saying good night and neck awhile?"

Sarah laughed. She also languished in the sharp sting of excitement.

"This is serious, Braden," he scolded, trying to maintain a grave expression that seemed determined to slip away. "We've never really necked, you know. What if we're not compatible?"

"That does sound serious."

"Damned right it is," he agreed, grabbing her by the wrist and pulling her against him as he fell back into the corner of the sofa. Her hands flattened against his solid, broad chest.

He kissed her forehead, the tip of her nose, the indentation below her nose, her lips, her chin.

"If we're going to *neck,* don't you think you ought to pay some attention to my *neck?*" she asked dreamily.

"You've got a point," he murmured, tilting his head and nibbling a trail from her earlobe to the hollow of her throat. There, he drew a moist design with the tip of his tongue.

Sarah giggled. "It tickles," she accused.

"I'm not trying to be funny. I'm trying to be sexy," he growled, sounding highly offended, but when he pulled back, there was laughter bubbling in his eyes. Cade's smile slowly faded as he slipped the pad of his thumb to her bottom lip and rubbed back and forth. "I can't believe you're really in my arms."

"I can't either." Swallowing hard, she added, "It isn't wrong, is it, Cade?"

"Does it feel wrong?"

Without hesitation, she shook her head. "No."

"Is isn't wrong, Sunshine. Nothing that feels this right can be wrong." His head dipped, his lips leisurely working against hers in a honey-wet kiss. "Tell me one of your fantasies," he ordered as his mouth played sexy games with hers.

"What?"

"You said you had wild fantasies of me. Tell me one."

Rose-colored warmth flushed Sarah's cheeks. "Forget I said that," she groaned.

"Hey," he said, raising her suddenly lowered chin with a finger, "are you going shy on me?" At her embarrassed silence, he encouraged, "Tell me. Just one."

Her eyes met his, then scurried away.

"Sarah," he said coaxingly, so coaxingly she heard herself answering.

"Tonight . . . when we were in the kitchen . . ."

He waited. "Tonight, when we were in the kitchen what?"

She hesitated, at last screwing up her courage, though her eyes didn't quite meet his. "I fantasized that you weren't . . . that you weren't wearing underwear." At the admission, she grimaced and tried to bury her face in his chest, but he wouldn't let her.

"Sarah Braden!" he chastised in mock shock. "That's decadent."

"I know," she agreed, closing her eyes so she could at least hide behind that refuge.

"Wonderfully decadent," he amended, drawing her face to his and kissing her closed lids. "I hate to disappoint you, Sunshine, but I'm wearing underwear. See?"

His breath was but a fan against her eyelids when he took her hand and brought it to his thigh. He eased her hand beneath the slightly gaping fabric of his yellow shorts. He encouraged her fingers to crawl upward over muscle and the smooth curve of his hip until they brushed a leg band of elastic, then grazed the softness of cotton knit. Sarah's heart stopped seconds before it burst into a faster rhythm.

"That feels good," he murmured thickly.

"Yes."

"So good," he said as her hand splayed across his abdomen, her little finger only inches from an exquisite intimacy. Long seconds were devoted to tactile sensations and fluttery heartbeats.

"Tell me your fantasy," she said finally, breathlessly, as she withdrew her hand. She'd wanted to touch more of him, he'd wanted to be touched, but neither had forced the moment.

"Which one?" he asked, the words unsteady. "I have so many."

"Any one," she insisted, her eyes now locked with his.

He didn't hesitate, wasn't at all shy in his answer, and that alone made what he said seem sensual beyond words. "You're lying above me, the way you are now, and I'm touching your breasts."

The air suddenly fled Sarah's chest.

"I want to touch you so badly," he whispered. The back of his hand feathered against the globe of one breast as it hid beneath her plaid blouse. Her breath caught in reaction. "I want to see you, kiss you . . ."

Sarah sighed as he inched upward and found the hollow of her throat with his lips, lips that slowly moved down to the V of her blouse. He nuzzled that spot, warming it with his uneven, vaporous breath. When his fingers fumbled at the first button, she sighed again.

"Cade."

"Is that a Cade-yes or a Cade-no?" he asked huskily.

"Yes . . . yes," she answered with an impatience that startled her.

The buttons opened, one after heart-stopping one. With hands that suddenly shook, he tugged the blouse from her shorts and unhurriedly pulled it wide. Lying between his legs, her hands propped on the arm of the sofa, she felt his scorching gaze rove over the filmy beige lace confining her breasts. His finger rose, paused, then traced the inner swell of each breast, his thumb finally grazing, with excruciating softness, the already hardened peak of one beneath the dainty filaments of lace.

At the delicious ache, Sarah whimpered, and he released the front clasp of her bra, freeing her breasts to tumble forward as if reaching toward him. His hands—even the one encased in the cast—worshiped, adored, idolized.

"Is the cast scratching you?" he asked, his voice gritty with passion as he kneaded her fullness in a gentle caress.

"No," she answered in what voice she could find.

"Oh, Sarah," he whispered, "not even in my wildest dreams . . ." The accolades ended when his mouth connected with the object of his praise. The tip of his tongue circled one dark nipple, round and round, moist and hot, shooting sparks through her that threatened to make her explode. She writhed in glorious agony as he took the brown bud into his mouth. He sucked, tugged, laved until she thought she would scream.

"Cade!" she moaned as her arms buckled under the weight of her emotions.

He quickly glanced up into her face. Her eyes were closed, her neck arched, her breathing coming through parted lips. With movements sure and swift, he pulled her to him and rolled her onto her back on the sofa. Their positions reversed, he now rested in the cradle of her legs. He stared down into her face with intense, passion-hued eyes. But he stared with something more: with disbelief, with awe, with an emotion so tender it brought tears to her eyes.

"Sarah," he whispered, his mouth claiming hers.

The kiss was a dichotomy: sweet and loving, yet passionate and flaming with desire. His shirt had worked free of his shorts, merging the bare skin of his chest with the bare skin of hers. Breasts tunneled into wiry sprigs of hair, bringing a note of pleasure deep from his throat. An instinctive rhythm began—hips seeking to lose themselves in hips of the opposite gender. Cade thrust forward; Sarah responded. Sarah thrust upward; Cade responded. Both groaned.

Suddenly he stopped and lay perfectly still as he dragged his mouth from hers. As if boneless, he dropped his head, his lips resting near her ear. Threading his fingers through her hair, he struggled to corral his runaway breath. Minutes labored by, both fighting for a control that seemed always just beyond reach. Finally, Cade pushed from her and moved to sit on the edge of the sofa. He pulled his knit shirt down over his heaving chest.

"Cade?" She spoke softly, joining him in a sitting position and covering her breasts by hugging the blouse to her.

His eyes met hers. "Not yet, Sunshine."

She studied him, both with her eyes and her heart. She shook her head. "No, not yet." She started to say something else, but he interrupted her.

"Go to bed." When she didn't comply, he added, "Please?"

The last image she had of him was his hand raking through his hair as he slumped back into the sofa. The last image he had of her was her walking from the room with a slightly confused look in her beautiful gray eyes.

He'd never be able to stop again, Cade thought as he let the male ache wash over him in frustrating ripples of pain-pleasure. He didn't know how he had stopped this time. He'd waited so long to feel her beneath him, alive with a passion he'd inspired, and the moment he had, he'd stopped, leaving her about as confused as he.

Why had he stopped?

He took a deep, cleansing breath. The answer was simple . . . and complicated. He had stopped because he was uncertain she was ready for this level of commitment. He was uncertain she'd come far enough in her thinking yet, and he'd waited too long—too damned long in nights too damned dark—to settle for anything less than everything she had to give. And then there was David. A sharp pain gored his heart. He had to tell Sarah about David's still loving her. Had he really thought he could keep it from her? If he had, he had been wrong. Any future that he and Sarah might have together had to be based on truth. He couldn't, wouldn't, play second best to his brother. And he wouldn't cheat Sarah. If she wanted David back . . .

He couldn't complete the thought. Oh, Lord, how could he tell her? How could he gamble the sweet taste of her breasts, the sweeter feeling of her body moving beneath his?

How could he gamble the fact that he might never feel that sweetness again? Might never know it in its completeness?

Sarah experienced an acute sense of relief when, Wednesday of the following week, as she was reading the phone messages forwarded by Mrs. Babish, Cade announced he was wanted in Dallas that afternoon. Since Saturday night, the house had jumped with an electrifying tension that had left both of them emotionally drained. Their relationship had reverted to a nontouch status. Each seemed to sense they would never again be able to stop the passion that had erupted on the sofa, so both were extremely careful to begin nothing. She knew that Saturday evening had ended correctly, but she kept asking an endless round of questions: Would she have stopped him? Why had *he* stopped? And just how long would it be before desire obliterated all reason?

They left Gilmer shortly after noon under threatening rainclouds. With each passing mile, the sky grew more sullen until, at a spot just north of their goal, the heavens, now as black as the fertile Texas soil, ripped open and spilled forth buckets of fresh, late-August rain.

Some forty minutes later, the windshield wipers slashing back and forth at top speed, she dropped Cade under the portico of a multistoried office building.

"I'll be a couple of hours," he said, breaking a silence that had gone on for miles.

"Fine. I'll swing back by"—she checked her watch—"about four-thirty." He opened the van door. "Cade?" He glanced up. "Don't forget Ms. Mona," she said with a half smile she hoped would leave them on a happier note.

His lips arced into the other half of her smile. "I won't." Slipping from the seat, he immediately turned back to her with a face now etched in concern. "Be careful."

She nodded and watched as he shut the door and walked the short distance into the building. The navy suit and red knit tie he wore made him look so . . . so handsome, she thought. And so sexy. But then, everything he'd said and done since Saturday was sexy—the kind of sexy that was responding poorly to cold showers. She leaned her forehead against the steering wheel. Oh, heavens, where was all this leading? Where did she want it to lead?

The impatient honk of a horn behind her shelved the issue. But it was only that, she knew: the shelving of an issue that she was soon going to have to face, that they both were going to have to face.

She spent the afternoon meeting with Mr. Ambrezzi, who was delighted with her plans for his yogurt shops, and with two new clients. All the while Cade was only one thought removed from her mind. What was he doing? Was he thinking of her? Was he missing her? At four-forty she pulled the van back under the portico. Cade immediately appeared.

"I was getting worried," he said as he slid in beside her. A blowing rain whipped in with him.

"I'm sorry. It's the weather. How'd everything go?"

"Pretty good. Still negotiating, though. They said they'd let me know something soon."

White sheets of rain lashed across the windshield, and thunder, low and menacing, growled in the near distance. A bolt of lightning streaked across the sky right before them, brightening a late afternoon that was already turning the shade of charcoal.

"The weather's getting worse," Cade stated, loosening his tie. "Why don't we stay here tonight and drive back in the morning?"

Sarah's eyes darted to him. She wasn't certain why her heart skipped a beat, but it did. Maybe it was because they would be staying overnight in the same city with David. Maybe it was because her house was so much smaller than Cade's, so much more intimate, so much harder for two people to stay in and not touch.

Cade's hand hesitated at his tie. "You can drop me at a motel," he said, reading her mind or at least her reaction.

Sarah pulled the van out into the stream of traffic that was sloshing its way along at a snail's pace. "No," she heard herself say, questioning her wisdom even as she did so. "We'll stay at my place."

* * *

The house emanated musty desertion and cloying hot-
ness. Cade immediately turned on the air conditioning, sending a cool air to stir the fine layer of dust that seemed
everywhere, even on the broad leaves of a rubber plant
desperate for moisture. Sarah watered it, making a mental
note to remind Mrs. Babish to give it occasional attention.
While Sarah scoured through the slim offerings of her pan-
try, Cade looked around the house, finally settling on the
sofa with a back issue of *McCall's*.

They talked of inconsequential things because neither
wanted to speak of what was really on their minds: the fact
that they were spending the night together in this very small
house, the fact that they wanted to touch each other more
than they wanted to breathe another breath, the fact that the
storm outside seemed calm by comparison to the one raging
inside.

Dinner was compliments of the freezer: a frozen pizza
and vanilla ice cream. Appetites proved fair, conversation
poor. Afterward, Cade cleared the table and Sarah washed
the few dishes. As he reached around her to slip the ice
cream bowls into the cabinet, his shoulder brushed hers.
She flinched; he pulled away quickly and immediately vacated the confining kitchen. Minutes later, Sarah found him
staring out the front window at the driving rain. Careful to
keep a safe distance, she joined him, and silently they watched
as rain was joined by the clunk of marblelike hail.

"It's hailing," she said unnecessarily.

His gaze shifted to her. She had the sudden, curious
feeling—a feeling she'd had off and on since Saturday—
that he wanted to tell her something. "Yeah, it's hailing,"
he said instead, cursing himself for not having the courage
to tell her about David's wanting her back. If he didn't do
it soon, he was going to lose his mind. And if he did, he
might lose Sarah . . . even before he'd ever had her.

"You want to play chess?" she asked.

"No, not tonight."

"Cards?"

"No."

"Want to watch TV? I think—"

"No."

What do you want to do? Her unspoken question darted about the room and was answered in the same unspoken fashion. *I want to make love to you.*

Cade ultimately broke the inches-thick tension with, "I think I'll go shower, then sack out on the sofa for the night. We need to leave early in the morning."

"The sofa's short," Sarah said in apology.

Cade smiled, the first smile she'd seen that evening. "I'll take a short nap."

The tilt of his lips, as always, did strange things to her. It also made her smile, which she was still doing as she watched him walk from the room. Minutes later, when she heard the shower running, she tried to divert her attention with activity. She changed into a pair of faded jeans, found fresh linen and a pillow for the sofa, and sat down to record her telephone messages from the answering machine. She was just taking down information about two prospective clients when a third message blared forth.

"Sarah? This is David." Sarah stopped writing. "I . . . uh . . . I've tried to call you several times. I keep getting this damned machine. Just wanted to say hello. I'll try to get back to you."

Sarah frowned, at the same instant swinging her gaze to a noise in the doorway. Cade, his suit pants back on, his white shirt hanging open following the shower, stood staring at her. His face was a portrait of pain.

"David," she explained. "He called to say hello." Even as she wondered what David wanted, she was questioning the intense look in Cade's eyes.

"He wants you back," Cade said calmly, too calmly.

Her forehead furrowing, she queried, "Wants me back? What do you mean?"

Cade stepped into the room, walked past her, and returned to the window to stare out. "He thinks he's still in love with you," he said blandly as he propped his uninjured hand against the window frame. "Hell, maybe he is!" His sudden burst of anger seemed directed at David, himself, and maybe even Sarah for making him care so deeply.

"What are you talking about?" she asked, moving from the sofa to stand beside him.

He glanced down at her. "After he took me to lunch, he talked about the counseling and . . . you. He told me he isn't over you. He wants you back. I should have told you then, but . . ." The words seemed torn from him, leaving him bleeding with emotion.

Sarah categorized David's wants as totally unimportant when compared to Cade's obvious pain and guilt. She reached out to comfort him, but he drew back as if he didn't deserve her understanding, her solace.

"I should have told you," he repeated, adding hoarsely, "but I couldn't."

Her hand settled on his arm. This time he didn't shy away. "Cade, I don't want him back. It's over. I wish him well, but I don't want him back. I'm not in love with him."

Cade's eyes were searching, his breath loud in the silence.

"Are you sure of that?" he asked almost inaudibly.

"Yes," she said, her voice strong.

"Sarah, for godsake be sure. I don't think I could stand—"

"I've never been more certain of anything."

And she hadn't. She knew beyond a doubt that she didn't want David Sterling, just as she knew beyond a doubt that she wanted Cade. Wanted him as her friend, wanted him as her lover. She wanted him in every way a woman wants a man in her life. She didn't care that some might see their relationship as improper, and, God forgive her, right this moment she didn't even care if she came between brothers. She just wanted Cade. Wanted him to hold her, kiss her, ease this gnawing, impatient ache.

"Go to bed," Cade ordered roughly as if he had just spent his last penny of self-control.

Lightning flashed like yellow-white ribbons while thunder clashed, angry god against angry god. Cade and Sarah stood, watching each other, waiting, silently pleading.

"Cade . . ."

His heart burst at the softness of her voice.

"... love me."

Her words were lost in a clap of thunder, but Cade understood them as clearly as if she'd shouted them from a mountaintop. Understood them, cherished them, and trembled at their beauty.

CHAPTER SEVEN

GOLDEN LIGHT GLOWED from the bedroom lamp. Rain pummeled, fistlike, against brave windowpanes. The clean scent of showered male intermingled with feminine perfume, creating an intoxicating fragrance and casting a seductive spell over the man and woman who stood, mere feet apart, waiting . . . wanting . . .

Sarah swallowed nervously. She'd never experienced the emotions now coursing through her. She'd never felt this wanting, this ravenous needing, nor this uncertainty as to how to go about easing the want, the need. She'd never been a shy lover, but then, she'd never made love with Cade, never made love with a man who was once her brother-in-law, never made love with her best friend.

Cade's eyes, slumberous with passion yet alert with sensitivity, swept her face, reading there her hesitancy, her uncertainty. Pain frosted the blue of his irises.

"Sarah, are you sure you want this?"

"Yes," she answered without hesitation, hastening to voice the sudden, unpleasant thought that had just sprung into focus, "Are you?"

"Yes," he said, cutting through her doubts in a strong though ragged voice. "I've wanted to make love to you for so long that it seems forever." He expelled a long, desire-broken sigh. "I haven't been with a woman since I kissed you at the hospital."

She heard the words, but their full meaning came in slow bits and pieces that, when meshed together, curled contentedly about her heart.

"You haven't?"

He shook his head. "No. I didn't want anyone but you."

"Oh, Cade," she whispered.

"I still want only you."

Emboldened by his admission and her passion, Sarah's hand moved from her side to the first button of her blouse. She worked to unmoor it, but her fingers shook so badly that she had to stop and try again.

Cade stepped forward, quieted her hand by taking it in his, brought it to his mouth, and kissed her clenched knuckles.

"You're trembling," he accused, the words warm against the back of her hand. "I don't want you to tremble. Not because of me."

"Part of it is because I want you so badly," she said truthfully, her eyes shadowed with desire as they met his.

"And what's the other part?"

"I feel . . ." She stopped.

"What do you feel?"

"A little awkward . . . I mean, you and I . . . we've always been either family or friends."

"I know. I feel it, too."

"You do?"

He nodded. "But I want you, need you, not like family or a friend." His eyes, deep blue and hazed with the fever coursing through his veins, bore into hers. "I want you as a lover. Can't we just be a man and a woman who want each other? Does it have to be so complicated?"

Did it? she thought, answering both him and her by pulling her hand from his. This time, the buttons of her blouse fell prey to a surer touch, one ablaze with conviction. The blouse, already hanging free of her jeans, slid open, a mirror image of Cade's dangling shirttails. As she released the clasp of her bra, she saw his eyes cloud to the color of a midnight caress. She heard his breath drawn from his chest with a corrugated silkiness.

"Oh, Sarah," he whispered, reaching for her.

His hand eased to the back of her neck, and with fingers spread wide, he drew her against him, his mouth covering hers with moist urgency. Her body fit to every sleek curve of his even as her mouth flowered to his kiss like a rose that can bloom only at the right ray of sunlight. She budded, she blossomed, she opened the petals of her mouth to his tender insistence. His tongue filled her, imbuing her with his heady taste, sending her senses staggering. She moaned, slipping her hands into the folds of his shirt, where her palms flattened against the hair-roughened wall of his warm chest.

Even as she sought to know every contour of his chest—solid muscle, downy hair, the enticing way chest slid into stomach—he raked the blouse from her shoulders, dragging the thin straps of her bra with it, and abandoned both garments to the floor. His good hand cupped one breast, while he ran the exposed fingertips of the other hand ever so gently back and forth against the nipple of the other. Flickers of fire burst into being, sending flames licking along her nerves.

"Oh, Cade," she moaned, swaying into him, "it's been so long . . . so long."

His arms went around her, securing her tightly against him. With careful movements, he shed his shirt as he held her, bracing her with one arm, then the other. Finally, he settled her chest to his—soft peaks and womanly curves flush against hardness and hair—and for long moments neither spoke. He simply held her while she held him.

But desire proved a greedy master.

With unspoken agreement, their hands wandered to waistbands—his to hers, hers to his. He unsnapped; she unsnapped. He unzipped; she unzipped. His eyes riveted to hers, he peeled the faded jeans from her legs and stooped—she bracing her hands on his shoulders—to pull them from her entirely. That done, he removed his own pants and left them where they lay.

Sarah's senses spun at the beauty of his body. His shoulders were so wide, his chest so masculinely sculpted in hair, that the sight of him sent her heart thundering in the same way that thunder boomed and rumbled just beyond the window. And his legs, his thighs, his ... Her eyes stopped, mesmerized by the briefly cut underwear shielding a male body that blatantly declared its need, its long-denied need. Breath quivered at her parted lips.

"Take them off," he whispered, his eyes burning into hers with a bold, elemental need.

Her heart, beating so erratically moments before, jammed into a faster pace that left her dizzy. But not so dizzy that she didn't step closer in answer to his plea. Her fingers brushed his briefs, then slid beneath the elastic waistband, her palms resting flat against the side of each hipbone. She paused and became aware that his fingers were poised at the folds of lace hugging her hips. His intention was clear: What she did to him, he would perform in silken duplication. The realization sent rays of excitement racing through her to gather in a spot very near where his fingers were currently taunting with their touch.

She rolled the fabric down even as her own lacy panties fell away; she slid her hands to his buttocks, where she tugged the cotton over the swell of his hips. Muscles tightened beneath her hands, and she wondered if he felt her muscles tightening beneath his. Holding her breath, she eased the briefs down in front, their descent momentarily impeded by the strength of his arousal. At last, his underwear pooled at his feet just as hers slithered floorward. Both stepped from the scraps of material.

"Are you all right?" he asked.

"Yes. Are you?"

A tiny smile nipped a corner of his mouth. "I'm in no condition to know." The hint of humor ebbed away. He reached for her hand—both his and hers were now trembling—and brought it to his lips. He kissed her palm, then kissed it again. "Touch me," he whispered hoarsely, pushing her hand lower, lower. "Touch me the way I've dreamed of a million times."

As her hand went where he led, she was vaguely aware that David had never asked this of her. She suddenly felt both cheated and relieved—cheated because Cade had just made her intimate touch seem the most treasured thing in the world, relieved because it was a treasure she knew she wanted to share only with this man.

He was warm, hard, pulsing with need. Her hand was burning, stinging, stroking in an instinctive rhythm she ceased to be mistress of.

Cade moaned, arching himself against her tempting fingers. And then, strong, powerful arms swept her off her feet and placed her with gossamer gentleness in the middle of the bed. The eyelet spread seemed incredibly sensual to her bare skin, but she dimly reasoned that anything, everything, would seem sensual at this moment. To prove the point, Cade's weight crushed the mattress, and heated vibrations darted through every cell of her body.

But she soon realized that they were pale vibrations compared to those created by his kisses. When his mouth claimed hers, she thought she might die from sheer ecstasy, and she really didn't care if she did.

"You taste better than any dream," he whispered thickly as his mouth deserted hers for a tanned shoulder, then trailed to her neck, which she slanted to help him in his slow, wonderful torture of her. But he'd only begun to ply her with kisses. He rained them randomly over earlobes, fingers, palms, toes, soles, navel, and breasts. And filled in all the gaps with small, close kisses that left her feeling as if she'd been carpeted in flowers from head to toe. When his mouth traveled to her stomach, and lower, she gasped. The liberties he took were liberties David had never taken, liberties David had never wanted to take, liberties she was certain wouldn't have felt this right with any man but Cade.

"Cade . . ." she whispered, her hips restlessly straining against the velvet torment of his mouth.

His eyes melding with hers, he stretched the length of her and, grimacing from the weight accepted by his injured wrist, wordlessly bound them as one. Slowly, he filled her;

slowly, she received him into her body. Both sighed and
fought for breath. Both thought the moment as close to
heaven as they'd ever been.

"Sarah," he whispered, not moving but devouring her
with eyes of tenderness. "My Sarah . . . You were always
mine . . . always."

"Yes," she whispered, knowing, feeling the truth of his
words. "Always."

His lips found hers, sharing with her her intimate taste
and sharing also the promise of love. This time when their
hips stirred, both knew there would be no cessation until
that perfect moment of physical peace. Outside, the storm
raged, but it was a weak display of emotion compared to
the love music singing softly off the bedroom walls. Cade
praised her, adored her, pleased her until her only goal
became to praise, adore, and please him.

At that splendorous moment, when all the world receded
to insignificance, Sarah cried. Cried because she'd never
really made love until that night. Cried because she'd wasted
two years with David. Cried because she'd wasted so many
years without Cade.

She wasn't certain, but she thought Cade cried as well.

Ragged breathing slowly returned to an even cadence.
Bodies stilled and quieted and slipped into a state of blissful
lethargy. The night hummed with the lulling sound of gentle
rain and lovers' sighs.

Sharing the same pillow, their faces so close that their
breaths mated, they lay with lips swollen, bodies love-sated,
and hearts brimming with emotions tender and fragile. Each
watched the other with eyes of contented wonder.

Cade stretched out his disabled arm, his fingers grazing
the puffiness of her bottom lip before rolling the sensitive
flesh to trace the outline of her teeth. Carefully capturing
the sensual invader, Sarah kissed each fingertip where it
extended from the white plaster of the cast.

"Did you hurt your wrist?" she asked.

His lips quirked naughtily. "I had a more pressing ache
to consider."

"I'm sorry," she said, kissing his little finger and sending belated shivers through his body and hers.

"About the more pressing ache?" he teased.

A suggestion of color seeped into her cheeks. "No," she said with a smile, "I'm sorry about your wrist." As she spoke, she nuzzled her cheek against his hand like a snuggling kitten. She closed her eyes, luxuriating in the feel of cast and skin and Cade.

"You cried," he said throatily.

She opened her eyes, smoke-gray and still misty from their lovemaking. His eyes shone the deep blue of concern.

"Yes," she answered.

"Because it was good, or because it wasn't?"

"Do you have to ask that?"

He studied her and remembered—remembered the way she had clung to him, the way she had moved so uninhibitedly beneath him, the way she had gasped his name, dragging it out in wispy slivers of sound.

"I cried because I've never felt that way before."

"What way?" he asked.

"As if I were somehow lost, as if I somehow became you and you became me." She gave a small, embarrassed smile. "Does that make any sense?"

He brushed back a strand of raven hair from her eyes. "Oh, yes," he answered as if he understood completely.

"And I cried," she added, lowering her eyes from his, "because all these years I'd never known to cry. David never . . . no man ever made me feel that making love could be so beautiful that you'd want to cry about it."

His fingertips tilted her chin up until her eyes connected with his, blue and gray meeting with no reserve, no disguise. "I never . . ." He swallowed. "I never knew it could be that way either." With that, he pulled her to him, wrapping her in a close embrace. Her arms folded about his back, her cheek cozying to his hair-sprigged chest, while his cheek rested against the top of her head. Their bare bodies meshed at every point, man to woman, woman to man.

It felt so right to be in his arms this way, she thought. So right. And that realization made her feel a little guilty.

It should have felt this right with her husband, but it hadn't. Had David sensed that their loving had fallen short of this perfection? Had he known it could be this right, and that he or she, or both, didn't feel it in their marriage? Had this driven him into the arms of other women? No, she consoled herself; David's preoccupation with other women had left him unable to assess the status of their marriage. He'd been too busy with extramarital affairs to notice any dissatisfaction she was feeling, any imperfection their marriage contained. But then, she thought on another swell of guilt, maybe her own heart had been divided as well. Maybe even while married to David, she'd felt heart-stirrings for Cade.

". . . guilt."

She glanced up at the word so blamefully delivered, the word that so exactly echoed her own thoughts. The eyes Cade lowered to hers were glazed with the harsh look of self-reproach.

"I've felt such guilt about David. Do you have any idea the guilt you feel at wanting to make love to your brother's wife? Do you have any idea what it's like to die inside at the thought of his making love to her? Hating him for it but knowing he has every right?"

"Oh, Cade," she whispered, bracketing his face with her hands, "don't do this to yourself. You did nothing to feel guilty about."

"You remember the night the three of us went out to eat at Old Warsaw?" he asked, seemingly intent on self-punishment.

Sarah nodded. She remembered the night well; they'd been celebrating one of David's new business deals. What she remembered most, though, was being six weeks pregnant and slightly sick to her stomach. Or maybe she'd been sick to her stomach because she'd suspected her husband was still seeing other women.

"You looked so beautiful that night, even though you were sick." His recognition that she'd been ill, which she hadn't mentioned—and certainly David hadn't picked up on it—surprised her. "I wanted to hold you, comfort you, make love to you so badly," he said huskily. "Instead I watched as David took you home to hold you . . . comfort you . . . make love to you." His expression hardened. "I hated David that night . . . almost as much as I hated myself."

Sarah's thumbs smoothed the drawn tightness at his temples. "When we got home, we fought," she said, smiling sadly. "There was no comforting. And when he made love to me, it was in anger. It was the last time we made love."

Cade closed his eyes, and his breath rattled in his chest. With slow movements, she pulled his mouth to hers, where both tried with the feel of lips to heal, to erase, to exorcise the past.

"Oh, Sunshine," he murmured against the rose-soft folds of her mouth, "I didn't want to want you."

"No," she agreed, her lips seeking to bring his back to hers.

"I didn't want to want my brother's wife," he whispered, his lips now beginning to move in a fevered, tormented rhythm.

"No," she said, answering his desire with a burst of her own.

"But you're not his wife now," he said, his lips nipping, tasting, gently biting hers as fire thickened in his veins.

"No . . . not his wife." The words were wrenched from her and lost somewhere in the warmth of his mouth.

"I want you," he groaned.

"Yes," she groaned back, her body shifting against his in impatience.

"I need you."

"Yes."

"Say you want me," he begged.

"I want you," she said as his teeth took fierce little nibbles of her earlobe. "I need you," she added breathlessly, ribbons of desire chasing away all coherent thought. "I—"

His lips smothered the word, just as his body smothered hers as he rolled her to her back. He entered her swiftly but tenderly, and they made love with a thoroughness that paled all yesterdays. Each knew, however, that tomorrow lay on unknown, unplotted shores. But right that moment, the fu-

ture possessed no power; that resided only in the present.
And the present was murmured love words, the feel of him
moving inside her, the feel of her sheathing his strong sweetness, the feel of Sarah and Cade.

At the moment of his climax, he groaned her name against
her ear . . . and something she couldn't understand. She
couldn't understand the words but decided it didn't matter.
She felt the peace of their unspoken meaning.

Sarah stood in the kitchen savoring the morning aroma
of perking coffee. Forty minutes earlier, she had tumbled
from bed—leaving Cade asleep in a boy-man pose that had
brought a smile to her lips and a warmth to her heart—
showered, and slipped into a robe. She had then made her
way to the kitchen.

Leaning against the cabinet, she now stared out at the
Thursday morning rinsed clean and fresh by yesterday's
storm. The sun shone as a bright disk of energy just climbing
out of the horizon. A few scattered clouds, pink and plump,
remained, but only as a testimony to what had been, not as
a portent of something to come.

Sarah hugged her arms about her and wondered where
last night's peaceful feeling had fled. Peace. It was such a
quicksilver spirit. In Cade's arms she had felt nothing but
peace and the magic of their lovemaking, but this morning
that peace had been supplanted by fear, a nagging, slow-
twisting fear. Would he awake with regrets about last night?
Would they discover in the revealing light of day that a
friendship, as close and solid as any had ever been, had
been scarred, damaged, altered in some way that rendered
it less instead of more? Could friends become lovers and
still remain friends? The thought that perhaps they couldn't
left her with an emptiness in the pit of her stomach.

And even if friends could remain friends while being
lovers, this particular relationship was riddled with problems. Cade, for all his talk against David, still loved his
older brother. Just the way David loved him. Being close
to her own sister, she could identify with this special familial
bond and knew that she could never forgive herself for

coming between the two brothers. No more than they would forgive her. David's lack of forgiveness she could perhaps live with, but Cade's was another matter altogether.

The thought of her sister veered the course of her worrisome musings. Would her sister understand, approve of this relationship? Would the rest of her family? Her friends? She knew that she and Cade were leaving themselves open to criticism. Some would consider their involvement unfitting behavior, incestuous even, while some might be more unkind and hint that the relationship had been going on during her marriage.

And maybe it had, Sarah thought, once more wrestling with the ensnaring tentacles of guilt. Cade had already confessed to deep feelings for her while she was married, and she had always thought of him in special terms. Maybe in some faraway corner of her heart there resided feelings that she had thought best to hide from herself. But she could no longer hide them. Something was happening to her. Feelings were struggling against their bonds and threatening to make themselves known. That thought excited her. That thought scared her. That thought...

Strong arms slipped about her waist, dragging her flush against a male body. As she melted into the warm bareness of a chest, she closed her eyes on the heady realization that that elusive feeling of peace was back, that it lived somewhere in Cade's embrace.

"Good morning," he mumbled, nuzzling her neck with a chin in need of a shave. She found the scratchiness stimulating. It had been a long time since she'd experienced morning, man, and beard.

"Good morning," she returned, slanting her head for his kisses.

Once he'd had his fill of that special place between neck and shoulder, which left her weak, he turned her in his arms. Hers instinctively encircled his neck, while his hands sought the small of her back.

Both feasted on the sight of the other until tiny smiles crept to mouths that were all too willing to be merry.

"You look sensational in the morning," he said. "Of

course," he added, "you look kinda sensational at night."

"Kinda?" she queried, feigning irritation.

"Okay. You look knock-my-socks-off sensational at night."

"That's better," she said, smiling. They were kidding, teasing, acting like old and good friends. The thought lightened Sarah's heart, just as his broad smile did. "I'm afraid all I have to offer you is coffee," she said.

Cade's eyes lowered from hers to her lips. His smile faded. "Oh, I wouldn't say that."

His mouth claimed hers in gentleness, yet with that special sensuality of lips that were now familiar from a night of loving. His hands, lowering from her back to the swell of her hips, pulled her into the V of his legs. She sighed around a mouth performing delicious movements and brought her hands to cradle his stubbled cheeks.

"I need a shave," he said, his mouth only partially disengaging from hers.

"I like your beard," she returned, her palms stroking up and down.

"It's going, anyway," he said with a smile. "If you have a razor."

"I have one for my legs."

He grimaced. "The price a man pays for an assignation."

"Sorry," she teased back, "I don't have many lovers stay over."

"You'd better not," he growled, targeting her lips again. This time, he kissed, nibbled, and gently bit until streamers of desire unfurled in the windstorm of his touch. When the fingers of his plastered hand started unbuttoning her robe, the streamers fluttered wildly ... until she realized he was having trouble negotiating the buttons. She saw him grimace before switching to his other hand.

"Cade?"

"I think we broke my wrist again last night," he said. At the wounded look on her face, he threw in, "I'm only kidding, Sunshine. Honest. We just gave it a nice workout."

Two buttons had already given way under the expert ministrations of his left hand, and Sarah was preparing to pamper his right, when she suddenly frowned.

"Bambi?" she repeated, noticing for the first time the new autograph adorning his cast. Her eyes moved inquiringly to his.

Cade smiled devilishly. "The blond secretary at the toy company. She said she was a big fan of mine."

"How big?"

"Big enough that she cornered me and insisted on signing my cast."

"Did she now?" Sarah asked. "And what else did this big blond fan insist upon doing while she had you cornered?"

Cade's eyes sparked. "Why, Sarah Braden, are you jealous?"

"Maybe," she answered.

"I was hoping for something more along the lines of definitely," he teased. His mouth lowered to the gaping V of her robe and kissed the cleft between her breasts. He nuzzled the fabric aside and left feathery kisses on the rounded fullness. "Is a definitely too much to hope for?"

"No," she breathed into his hair. "It is definitely not too much to hope for a definitely." Minutes later, she sighed in languid contentment. "We are *definitely* not going to make it home at this rate."

Home. At the word, so drowsily delivered, Cade raised his head. He waited, probing her glazed eyes, but at last realized that she wasn't even aware that she'd spoken of going home while she stood in the middle of her own.

"No," he said, his tone softened by a wealth of emotion, "we're never going to make it home at this rate." He dipped his head for one last quick kiss. "I'm going to go take a shower."

The hiss of spraying water only slightly transcended Sarah's humming. So the relationship had problems, she thought, sliding into the oven some cinnamon rolls she'd found tucked away in the freezer. Any relationship has problems, right? No relationship was born to perfection, right? She was on the verge of responding in the affirmative when the doorbell rang. At almost the exact same instant, the shower stopped. With a frown and a quick look toward the bathroom, Sarah headed for the door, opened it, and found Mrs. Babish, her mouth poised for action.

"I told John I saw lights over here last night," came a sound the equivalent of a cannon's boom. As she stepped in, pushing past Sarah at a pace only one notch below a march, she hurled a volley of questions that left Sarah, if not the deliverer, breathless. "Well, tell me, are you back to stay? Is the job finished in Gilmer? Or are you going back? Do you want me to keep forwarding the mail? Tell me you didn't drive down in that horrendous storm."

Sarah blinked under the rapid-fire delivery.

"I told John I saw lights over here," the woman said again, cocking her hands on her hips and casting the conversation back to square one.

But not quite square one, Sarah thought, hearing Cade's footsteps heading in their direction. A wave of panic engulfed her.

"Mrs. Babish, I—" she began.

"Sarah, I can't find your raz . . . or." Cade stopped dead in his tracks. "Oh, I'm sorry. I didn't realize . . ."

Mrs. Babish, eyes wide in surprise, stared at the man before her; Cade, eyes narrowed in speculation, stared at the woman before him. Sarah closed her eyes and uttered a silent curse.

"This is my neighbor, Mrs. Babish," Sarah heard herself saying, and she marveled at the normalcy in her manner. "Mrs. Babish, this is Cade Sterling."

The older woman made a blatant survey of Cade, taking in his bearded face, his bare chest, the damp towel held in his right hand and leaving little doubt to his recent shower, and his feet peeking nakedly beneath the hems of wrinkled pantlegs. Like a general inspecting his troops, she turned her attention to Sarah, whom she seemed to see now for the first time since entering the house. Sarah could clearly hear the woman's mind ticking off her physical appearance—hair tousled, an indefinable sparkle in her gray eyes, love-flushed cheeks, lips that still looked swollen from passion's kiss, plus a robe unbuttoned past propriety. There was only one inescapable conclusion: Sarah had been well-loved—

recently—by the man standing at her side.

Reproach was settling on Mrs. Babish's face when recognition dawned. A smile slid across her mouth. "Sterling," she repeated. "I knew it. I knew you two would get back together. John and I almost divorced once, but—"

"No!" Sarah cut through her words, feeling her heart squeeze. "This is . . . David's brother."

The woman's eyes cut back to the man, roaming downward until they took in the cast visible beneath the towel.

"Brother?" she parroted, shock racing across her face. "You mean this is your *brother-in-law?*"

"Ex," Cade said in a meaningfully low growl.

Sarah said nothing. She simply eased to the edge of the nearest chair and watched as Mrs. Babish's chest swelled with sanctimonious disapproval.

CHAPTER EIGHT

IN THE QUIET roar that followed the closing of the door, Sarah sat motionless, still poised on the edge of the chair like a bird wishing for flight but procrastinating because it didn't quite know its destination.

"Damn!" Cade bellowed suddenly.

At his outburst, Sarah raised her eyes to him, just in time to see his fingers ravage his hair. Simultaneously, she realized her fingers were clenched in a tight fist at the neck of her robe. She released her hold and felt those fingers tremble uncontrollably.

"If tact were money," Cade growled, "that woman couldn't buy a loaf of bread."

"If morality were money," Sarah said, her voice devoid of emotion, "she probably thinks we'd starve, too."

At the truth of the words, Sarah grimaced. In all her life, she never remembered feeling such acute embarrassment, such overwhelming humiliation. Try as hard as she would to negate it, Mrs. Babish's censure threatened to taint the beauty of what she and Cade had spent the night sharing.

"Do you think what we did was immoral?" Cade stood quietly, his face set into inflexible lines of anticipation. His eyes flickered with a brooding quality.

119

Memories flashed through Sarah's mind—caresses as soft as love-spun satin; endearments whispered in shades of gold; breathing as pale as alabaster; and feelings so deep, so wide, so soaring, they slipped the bonds of her soul.

"Do you?" There was now a pointed urgency to the question.

"No," she said, shaking her head.

Cade closed his eyes, her answer washing over him like a soothing balm.

"But don't you see," she added, "that others will? Everyone will believe we're having a tawdry affair." The words forced a groan from her lips. "Oh, God, we are." She rushed a glance in Cade's direction. "Having an affair, I mean," she quickly amended.

He peered through thick lashes with eyes suddenly as hard as blue gemstones. "No, you mean tawdry, don't you?"

"I do not," she denied, appalled at his suggestion.

"I think you do." The words were low, biting, filled with an unkind judgment.

The accusation stung at Sarah's senses like hordes of marauding bees. At the obvious pain that crawled across her face, settling in an ashen-gray gaze that suddenly shimmered under the onslaught of tears, Cade's harsh expression melted.

She rose from the chair, regally. He stepped toward her, tentatively.

His hand grazed her arm in awkward communication. "Sarah, I—"

She jerked away from him, silencing his words, stopping his heart.

They stood staring at each other, each wondering how a night so perfect could have come to a moment so cruelly imperfect.

Had he been wrong about her feelings last night? he thought.

How could he believe she thought last night tawdry, when it had been the singular most wonderful night of her life? she thought.

How could she think our loving was immoral?

How could he think I thought our loving immoral?
Why hadn't she told her neighbor to go straight to hell?
Why hadn't she told Mrs. Babish to go to hell?
She pulled away from me!
Oh, God, I pulled away from him!
I want her!
I need him!
In the end, thoughts remained mute, wants and needs unfulfilled.

"I'll be ready in a few minutes," he said gruffly. "We need to get back."

"Yes," she answered, her voice equally stilted.

Watching as he turned and walked away, she stupidly thought, in the petty way the mind does during moments of distress, that the cinnamon rolls were probably ruined.

After trashing the charred cinnamon rolls and pouring the coffee into a thermos bottle, they left Dallas at seven thirty-five and commenced a journey that had no parallel in Sarah's experience. As uncommunicative as strangers, they traveled mile after lonely mile. Countryside Sarah usually admired, she now didn't even notice, and the music blaring from the radio, usually so enjoyable, she viewed as nothing but competition to her gloomy thoughts. When, thirty minutes into the trip, Cade reached over and impatiently snapped off the radio, Sarah gave a mental nod of approval. He obviously preferred his gloomy thoughts, too.

What were his bleak thoughts? she wondered, knowing, whatever they were, they were able companions to hers. Her thoughts were all tied up with one word: *anger*. She was angry with Mrs. Babish, angry with herself, angry with Cade. Angry with Mrs. Babish for her insensitivity, angry with herself for allowing the neighbor to spoil—even for a moment—the beauty of what happened between her and Cade, and angry with Cade for believing she regretted what had happened between them. She was also angry at herself for refusing the comfort, the apology, he'd offered. She had hurt him. But then, he had hurt her or she never would have pulled away.

Anger. Hurt. They were new components to her relationship with Cade. As friends, they'd never fought, never been angry with each other, never sat side by side without speaking, teasing, laughing. Did she have the answer to the question she'd asked just that morning? Was it impossible for friends to become lovers and still remain friends? The realization that she might, indeed, have her answer made her heart constrict in bitter agony. Oh, Lord, what would she do without Cade as a friend? What would...

Cade stirred, drawing Sarah's eyes to him and the thermos he held in his hands. Removing the cap, he awkwardly balanced bottle and cup and poured some of the hot black coffee, sending a pleasing aroma through the van's interior. The smell swirled around Sarah's nose, making her stomach grumble just as Cade took a sip of the brew. His eyes cut to her.

"Sorry," she said over yet another rumble of her stomach.

"Here," he said, shoving the cup toward her.

Controlling the wheel with her left hand, she reached for the cup, both she and Cade being almost comically careful not to brush fingers in the process. She put her lips to the spot where he'd drunk and took a swallow. The coffee tasted good; Cade tasted better. Her heart fluttered with memories of his lips pressed against hers, memories of his lips knowing her body—her breasts, the small of her spine, the soles of her feet, the dewy warmth of her waiting, aching femininity.

"Thank you," she murmured huskily as she passed the cup back to him.

He took it, placed his lips on the spot where Sarah's had been, and swallowed the last of the liquid. Sarah wondered if he, too, were tasting her the way she had tasted him... and, if so, whether pleasant, provocative memories had been stirred for him, too.

An hour later, the sight of the earth-sheltered house basking under a citron-yellow sun brought a rush of totally unexpected joy to Sarah. She'd been happy here in the past weeks, and now she felt as if she were returning to a haven of safety and protection. Her joy dimmed, however, when she realized that a house was nothing more than a structure, a collection of wood and cement and glass. It had no power to protect, to secure, to grant happiness. The reason she'd been happy here was because of a flesh-and-blood Cade, a man who had once been her friend, a man who'd recently been her lover, a man who might never be either again.

She parked the van and sat.

Cade remained motionless as well. Finally, he turned to her. "Sarah, I want to make one thing very clear." There was a calm steeliness to his voice that Sarah thought even more powerful than his anger. "I have no intention of apologizing for last night."

"Do you think I want you to?" she threw back, her tone threatening to adopt the anger he was so stridently avoiding.

He tossed the fast ball back into her court. "Do you?"

Her eyes shaded to the hostile gray of storm clouds, and the anger she'd felt all morning swelled to a bursting crescendo. "Damn you, Cade!" she hurled as she threw open the van door and started for the house.

Even before she made it to the front door, her stomach knotted and churned in nauseating twists and rolls. She had never, *never*, spoken to him so harshly, nor would she have believed she ever could. Moments later, standing in her bathroom, a cool cloth to her face and throat, she studied the woman in the mirror. What was happening to her? What was happening to Cade? What was happening to *them?*

Whatever was happening continued to happen. They worked side by side, neither saying more than the job required, and then went their separate ways. Cade spent the afternoon in the meadow, with maimed feelings and wounded thoughts, while Sarah tried to lay out a rough presentation for a new client. In a fit of exasperation, she finally gave up. She tried reading; she tried watching TV; she washed and dried a load of clothes, which depressed her even more when she saw Cade's shirts tumbling dry with her blouses, his underwear washing so intimately with hers. As a last resort to save her sanity, she went to the kitchen and prepared a dinner that both simply picked at with nonexistent appetites.

"I . . . uh . . . I think I'll turn in early," Cade said only a few minutes past seven o'clock.

"Yeah," Sarah agreed, grazing his eyes as she stood. "I need to wash my hair . . . and . . . uh . . . and do some things."

She did wash her hair, and the "some things" she did was sit in bed, her back propped against the headboard, her knees drawn to her chest and banded by her arms. She listened to the muffled noises that crept from Cade's room—his shower running, his closet door sliding open and closed, something falling and Cade's swearing.

At 10:05, the house quiet, she slipped from her room and went to the kitchen for a drink of water. As she came back down the hall, she noticed that Cade's bedroom door was open. Even as she watched, he stepped to the door to close it. Their eyes met and held, as if neither possessed the power to break the contact.

He wore only a pair of tight jeans that hugged his hips in a sexy manner. His feet were bare, as was his chest, and it was to the latter that Sarah's eyes uncontrollably roamed. Golden-brown hair, the feel of which still lived in her mind, teased her, while muscle and bone and sinew taunted her with memories so vivid, her breath grew sparse, her heartbeat heavy.

His eyes roved, too—over the gown he'd seen her in weeks before with such disastrous results to his libido. The gown's effect tonight was no less powerful, and he fought to drag his eyes from the shadowy spots where sheer white cloth rested against dusky-dark nipples. He finally succeeded in meeting her eyes again, and this time he forced a dispassion he didn't feel. Then, slowly, deliberately, he closed the door. The last thing he saw was pain streaking through her eyes.

For long, heartbreaking moments, Sarah stared at the barrier, a barrier she knew was far more than physical. As she stood there, she felt the shriveling death of something deep inside her. This time when she went to bed, she cried.

Cade leaned against the door, drawing in bottomless, unsatisfying breaths. Why had he done that? Why had he closed the door, effectively erecting a wall between them?

She had looked so hurt, so defenseless, like a wounded deer in hostile woods. And it had been he who had wounded her. Why? Dammit, because she'd wounded him! Hurt him! And, rightly or wrongly, he wanted her to hurt as badly as he was! With one sharp blow he drove his right hand against the door. Pain shimmered through his wrist and up his arm, and he sucked in another agonized breath. A smile contorted his face into a grim mask. The pain had served its purpose. For one brief second, the agony in his wrist had been greater than the agony in his heart.

> *The clock in the living room began its* bim-bam *announcement of midnight. Intermingled with the tin-tinnabulation came the sound of distant and hazy musk-rat voices.*
> *"Why are they deliberately hurting each other?" the feminine voice inquired.*
> *"Because each has been hurt," explained the patient, resonant tone of a male muskrat. "Unfortunately, human beings hurt in a pattern known to be the most perfect of circles. They are hurt, they seek to hurt those who hurt them, but then, the pain they inflict circles back to them because they can't stand to see those they love hurt."*
> *"How confusing," the feminine voice concluded.*
> *"How human," the male voice philosophized.*

The night either heals a hurt or makes it fester. For Sarah and Cade, the darkling hours held no curative powers. Both arrived in the studio the next morning irritable from no sleep and with emotions bone-raw. Sarah had but one goal—to get the daily strip finished and flee back to the sanctuary of her room—while Cade thought no further than of losing himself in his work.

"If you want coffee, you'd better get it now," he said, his tone blunt, his delivery brittle. "We've got a lot to do."

"I've already had coffee, thank you," she replied with a tartness she despised but couldn't seem to control. "And what is the 'lot' we've got to do?"

"I want to redo what we did yesterday."

"What's wrong with it?"

"In a word, everything."

Prickles of irritation shimmied over Sarah's tired body. "They why didn't you tell me that yesterday?"

"Because I didn't know it until today. See here?" he demanded, practically shoving the completed panel under her nose, "The ink hasn't held, Ms. Mona looks like a reject from a fat farm, and the strip ought to be divided into four sections instead of three."

Sarah let out a disgusted sigh. She didn't see a single one of the problems he mentioned. What she did see was a man, in tight jeans and a sweat shirt, who looked tired but never more handsome, a man she'd never wanted to hold her more than she did at this moment. Her weakness angered her more than the redoing of a perfectly fine comic strip.

"All right," she said, snatching the paper from him. "We'll do it your way. After all, you're the boss." And my one-time best friend, she thought bitterly.

They worked nonstop from 9:30 to 11:45. They worked silently but with the awareness that each was not alone in the room. Vibrations skittered off desk and drawing table to pass again and again through bodies growing more tense by the minute. At 10:09 Cade reached for a ruler, leaving behind a spicy scent of cologne to shatter Sarah's thin concentration; at 10:28 Sarah destroyed Cade's breathing by passing so closely that her jeans skimmed his; at 11:16 the way Sarah's breasts filled her yellow-knit shirt started a physical ache so powerful and so obvious that Cade stormed from the room; at 11:32 he came back and devastated Sarah's senses because of the way the sun filtered through the skylight and gilded his hair a rich amber-brown.

Damn! she thought, working more frenziedly, knowing her only salvation rested in the fact that the strip was nearing completion and that she could soon take her wounded emotions and wayward feelings and hide them in her room.

Damn! Cade thought, knowing he no longer had any salvation. It had been worn as smooth as a stone subjected to the ageless flow of water. Salvation damned, he saw, felt, tasted, smelled, heard nothing beyond Sarah.

To compensate for her hurt and her need of the man hurting her, she resorted to anger.

To compensate for his hurt and his need of the woman hurting him, he resorted to anger.

"Here," she said, shoving the redesigned panel at Cade. She stood, ran her hands into the back pockets of her jeans, and waited for the approval that would release her from this unbearable torture and send her hurrying to her room. As she waited, shifting from one foot to the other, her eyes, of their own volition, trailed over his taut jeans, which hugged a body she knew so well and splayed tight over the very essence of his manhood. She jerked her gaze upward.

"It's still not right," he said, noticing far more the way her jeans stretched across her stomach, then molded long, slender legs in absolute perfection.

Sarah raised her eyes to the ceiling and held them there for several frustrated moments before lowering them back to Cade. "There's nothing wrong with that. There wasn't anything wrong with the other one."

Cade's eyes roved from hers to her breasts, which were heaving with poorly contained anger. "Since when do you know so much about cartooning?" he asked in retaliation at the swift desire flooding his body.

A harsh light flashed in Sarah's gray eyes. "And since when have you become such an insufferable bastard?" At the ugly word, her hand flew to her mouth. "Oh, Lord . . . I'm . . . I'm so sorry."

Forever dragged by with two people ensnared in its silence.

Suddenly Cade's shoulders slumped, his weary sigh escaping into a room that had grown congested with pain. "Don't apologize. I've been asking for it all morning."

"And I've been lying in wait to give it to you," she admitted.

They assessed each other for the span of countless heartbeats. Sarah finally eased a hand from her pocket and reached for the cartoon.

"Here, let me have it. I'll do it over."

"No," Cade said, abandoning the paper to the drawing board, "let's work on a new panel instead."

Sarah nodded. "Okay. What's the theme?"

"Apologies," he replied, his voice now soft, his eyes now dark with a new emotion. At the flash of surprise in Sarah's eyes, he added, "Rigby Rat and Ms. Mona have had a fight."

Feeling the first small lessening of the tightness around her heart, she asked, "And what was the fight about?"

"I don't think either of them could tell you." Cade suddenly seemed unsure. He looked down, he looked up, he cleared his throat. "A third party said something that upset them, and I think they took it out on each other. He said something about her regretting the night they'd just shared, and he thinks it might have made her angry. At least he hopes she's angry and not regretting the night."

"She's angry," Sarah said.

"Is that why she pulled away from him?" There was pain in the question.

"Yes, and she regretted it instantly, but it was . . . it was already done . . . and she was still angry."

Eyes delved and probed. Both were unaware that they'd moved closer until he now stood so near she could see the tiny red lines of fatigue networking his eyes.

"Why did you close the door?" she whispered, her words mere ghostlike stirrings of the air.

"Because," he said, his voice trembling, "I'm an insufferable bastard." Long moments passed. "Look, I think— I *know*—he wants to apologize, but . . . uh . . . he's not really sure how to go about it."

"Maybe she could help him," Sarah offered. "Maybe she'd even apologize herself."

"Would she? Help him, I mean?"

"Try her."

"Sunshine, I—" His voice cracked. "I'm sorry."

His apology was the headiest of nectars that spread through her with sweet relief. "I'm sorry, too," she said.

"I'm not apologizing for making love to you," he added

as if he wanted her to be sure of just what he was apologizing for.

"I don't want you to," she added quickly. "I never wanted you to."

The words spoken, neither seemed quite sure of what to do.

She waited.

He waited.

"Do you think," she began, her eyes fighting bleariness, "that you could . . . uh . . . that you could hold . . ."

He grabbed her, crushing her to him.

". . . me?" This last was absorbed by the massiveness of his chest.

They clung, trying to become one. Sarah's arms feverishly hugged the firm muscles of his back, while his hands cradled her head. She felt the cast hard and uncomfortable and thought it the most wonderful feeling in the world.

"I'm sorry," he repeated near her ear.

"I'm sorry," she whispered into the hollow of his throat.

"It was my fault," he added.

"No, it was mine."

"Maybe I've refused to see all the problems we're going to have to face," he said.

"To hell with the Mrs. Babishes," Sarah said, meaning it—at least for this moment when Cade's embrace blurred all rational thought.

When his lips swooped to hers, Sarah's bones melted under the fiery onslaught of his kiss. His lips ravaged one moment, stroked slowly the next, only to return to a greedy bonding that excited, soothed, apologized, and promised all at the same time. His tongue made hungry forays that she fed with her own hungry need.

"You taste so good," he breathed against the wetness of her mouth.

"Taste me again," she pleaded.

He did, this time with a thoroughness that drove them both wild with flaring passion. His mouth wooed, courted, opening wider, wider, then pulling back to take short, nibbling kisses, then opening wider, wider to tug her feelings down, down into a sensual vortex. She felt his body growing hard in the revealing jeans, felt her own body growing moist. Anger and hurt receded; warm sensations of desire prevailed.

"Did you sleep last night?" he asked, his lips taking tiny pecks at hers.

"No. Did you?"

"Uh-uh," he answered, adding, "Want to go to bed?" He drew back, looking at her with smiling blue eyes.

She returned his smile. "To sleep?"

The mirth in his eyes descended to his mouth. "Eventually."

"What about the strip?" she teased as she jerked her head in the direction of the drawing table.

They answered in unison. "What strip?"

The noonday sun glittered through the skylight, bathing the empty studio in toasted gold and illuminating the cartoon on the drawing board. In that second, the very observant would have seen two muskrats wink in a secret conspiracy. Wink and smile and dissolve into muskrat chatter.

The same sun lighting the studio streaked through the octagonal stained-glass window in the master bedroom, casting colorful prismatic designs on the bare bodies stretched out on the bed.

They lay face to face, Cade loving her with his tender look, she loving him with hers. Raising his head, he planted daisy-soft kisses on her eyebrows, eyelids, eyelashes, and the sensitive hollow at her temple. She felt his misty breath; he felt her dainty, dancing pulse.

"I thought I'd die without you last night," he said thickly.

"I thought I'd die without you," she breathed, forcing him back to the bed by rising above him to return his gentle kisses. Her lips brushed his forehead, his closed eyes, the ridge of his nose, his mouth.

He moaned, taking her mouth with his until their breathing became labored and scant. Weak, Sarah lay back on her side, content to devour him with hungering eyes.

He threaded his fingers through her ebony-black hair. "I love your hair," he said. "I love your eyes. Lord, I love your eyes."

"Do you?" she asked in the way a lover pleads for a lover's praise.

"Yes," he said, his fingers trailing along her shoulder. "And I love your shoulder ... and your throat ... and your breasts." His palm skimmed the heaviness of her breast and made circular movements over and over until she urgently arched into him. Cupping his hand, he kneaded, caressed, coaxed the hard brown nipple to an even more thrilling hardness.

Sarah moaned, letting the delicious sensations storm through her body to nestle deep in her womanhood.

"Does that feel good?"

"Yes," she whispered.

When his mouth joined his hand, Sarah shifted restlessly, then more restlessly as his tongue flicked expertly across the swollen peak. He bathed the flowered bud in warm moistness, drawing it into his mouth slowly, rhythmically. Sarah whimpered an indistinguishable accolade and wove her fingers through his hair.

"Good?" he whispered, his breath hot against the aching crest.

"Oh, Cade, what are you doing to me?"

"Loving you," he answered as he slipped his hand to her waist and down the length of her thigh. Running his hand to the back of her knee, he pulled her leg up over his. The move left her open and vulnerable and waiting for his touch, which, when it came, fingers sure and seeking, stole her breath and her sanity.

"Cade!" The word vibrated with desperation.

Kissing her breast again, he lay back on his side, his passion-blurred eyes finding hers. He inched lower, his stomach gliding over hers—warm flesh to warm flesh, hair to smoothness—as he aligned himself with her.

"Guide me in," he whispered, matching her desperation. Her hand slid down his hair-clouded chest, over his stomach, and lower through coarse wisps of hair to grasp the silky shaft of his desire.

At her touch, his eyes closed and his mouth opened. He called her name.

She eased him through soft folds to a dewy threshold. He paused, as if savoring the moment, finally thrusting upward to join them as lovers. Both moaned, disbelieving that such physical beauty, such emotional joy, could exist.

"You feel so wonderful inside me," she whispered, her hand still resting at the juncture of their coupled bodies.

"What do I feel like?"

"Like . . . like warm gold." He kissed her with the gentleness of a spring breeze frolicking through fields of flowers.

"You feel so good around me," he said.

"What do I feel like?"

"Like liquid gold." He kissed her again, sipping at her womanly sweetness. "Like precious liquid gold."

As his mouth settled over hers, his hand moved to the curve of her hip, where he arched her against him, initiating a primitive, elemental, beautiful rhythm. Thrust to thrust, kiss to kiss, love word to love word. Time sped and lingered, lingered and sped, on temporal wings of pleasure. Minutes—a lifetime—passed before a brilliant ecstasy reigned, shattering kaleidoscopic lights that merged and tore asunder and merged again the rainbow colors beaming through the stained-glass window.

"Don't ever . . . pull away from me again," he said fiercely, his emotions cresting the wave of his climax.

"No," she whispered, spears of delight consuming her. "Never."

Wrapped in each other's arms, they slept almost instantly. His last thought was that he didn't know how much longer he could go without telling her he loved her. Her last thought was that she'd never had these strong feelings for anyone— this total oneness, this union of body and soul, this contentment. Even knowing that the world might be ready to judge them—she felt a tug on her contentment—she wanted only to be here in Cade's arms. She didn't care about censure. She didn't care about right or wrong. She didn't care.

Caring was for another time.

CHAPTER NINE

SEPTEMBER DRIFTED INTO town like a gypsy, quietly but with occasional gaudy splashes of color that stole the verdant green of summer.

In the week and a half that followed the fight and the breathtaking reconciliation, Sarah and Cade, by silent and mutual consent, shared his bedroom. There, they made love, talked, laughed, and made love again . . . and again . . . and again . . . because neither seemed able to get enough of the other. The days were wonderful, the nights perfect, and only in rare moments did they allow the problems inherent in their relationship to spoil their idyll . . . and then, only until the other kissed the worries away.

One Tuesday afternoon, they packed a picnic basket with fried chicken and white wine and went to the meadow. Beneath the sprawling limbs of a giant oak tree, they spread a quilt and eased to its patchwork surface. They ate until they were replete, drank wine until they were giddy, made love until they were weak with pleasure and sated with feelings of warmth and togetherness. With the September breeze sighing secrets across their naked bodies, Cade picked late-blooming wild flowers and sprinkled them in Sarah's hair, on her breasts, on her stomach, and at the V of her legs. He them picked the flowers a second time, to both their delight and their undoing.

Thursday night they showered together. While Cade tried to keep his healing wrist out of the water—and it *was* healing now that he'd given up slamming it into doors— Sarah washed his hair. The gentle baby shampoo, however, ended up places for which the product had never been intended. Amid giggles and shouts and soap in both pair of eyes, Sarah "shampooed" his body. Male nipples protruded so enticingly from a snow-white froth of lather that she was forced to turn more and more attention to them, which only caused more and more attention to be lavished upon her breasts. In the end she had as much shampoo on her as did Cade. It was the first time Sarah had ever been made love to against the wall of a shower stall. It was the first time Cade had ever felt like endorsing a product.

They drove into nearby Longview Saturday night for a movie. As they were leaving the theater, they ran headlong into Mike Palmer and Joe-Bob Ross, both escorting dates. The fact that Sarah and Cade were holding hands brought a hushed moment of awkwardness. In true caught-with-a-hand-in-the-cookie-jar style, they immediately released their clasp. No one seemed to know quite what to say or do. Cade and Sarah exchanged a long and meaningful look before he draped his arm across her shoulders and she slid hers about his waist.

"Why the hell didn't you say so?" Mike said under his breath as the three couples started off for the local coffee shop.

That night Sarah and Cade made love with a new freedom and a glorious optimism. Not all the world was like Mrs. Babish!

This wondrous discovery under her belt, Sarah felt happier than she'd ever been. The following Wednesday, however, she made an even happier discovery, this one a revelation of the heart. This discovery also troubled her, because she knew it had the power to change her life forever.

"You're sure you don't mind?" Cade asked for the dozenth time that Wednesday morning.

"I don't mind," Sarah assured him for the dozenth time.

A car horn honked loudly in the front yard, followed by another impatient blast.

"There's Mike now," she said, straightening the wayward collar of Cade's blue shirt.

"I'll mail the strip while I'm in town. We're going to look at that office space Mike's thinking of renting, then we'll grab a bite of lunch; then—"

"Go!" Sarah insisted at yet a third blaring of the horn.

Cade's lips covered hers for one quick kiss, two quick kisses, followed by a third that was quickly losing its quickness. "I hate to be away from you for even a little while," he breathed.

"You'll live," she breathed back, adoring the feel of his mouth next to hers.

"I'll exist," he corrected, taking her lips in a fourth farewell. This time his tongue dueled salaciously with hers and slicked wickedly over the wet walls of her mouth.

The horn screamed another intrusion, which Cade met with a groan and a curse.

"Go," she whispered, but with an obvious lack of conviction.

Tearing himself from her, he did go. Afterward, the house seemed suddenly and dreadfully empty, and Sarah forced herself to the studio, where she worked on one of her freelance projects. At noon she stopped for a tuna sandwich but went immediately back to work. She was still in the studio, bent over the drawing board, when she heard the front door open. The house instantly shed its oppressiveness, and seconds later, she felt warm lips doing crazy, delectable things to the back of her neck.

"Have I ever told you how much I like your short hair?" he growled. "It allows me to bite the sexiest neck in town." His teeth gently played out the threat of his words.

She giggled at what his mouth was doing, at what he was saying, and just because she suddenly felt like giggling.

"Most men don't like short hair. They think it makes a woman look like a man."

"That," he said, his tongue feathering her earlobe and sending goose bumps exploding over her body, "is one thing I'd *never* mistake you for."

She swiveled on the stool, bringing her lips to within inches of his. Neither closed the gap; both were content to enjoy the pleasure of anticipation.

"Hi," she breathed on wispy wings of air.

"Hi," he said, his breath as diaphanous as hers.

"Did you have a nice time in town?"

"Nope. I missed you. Did you have a nice time here?"

"Nope," she replied, rubbing the tip of her nose against his. "I missed you."

"I hope you were devastated by my absence," he said as his lips finally dipped towards hers.

"I was," she barely had a chance to say before his mouth firmly took what she so generously offered. The kiss was long and heady, sending quivery sensations speeding up and down both spines. He moved so close that Sarah could feel, could smell, the warm sunshine captured in the cotton of his shirt. She could also feel and smell the arousing fragrance of man.

"You wanna fool around?" he teased when their mouths finally parted.

"Cade!" she cried, her fist playfully striking his chest. "That's the most unromantic thing I've . . ." She trailed off, her eyes lowering to his left hand, which he suspiciously held behind his back. "What have you got?"

"What makes you think I've got—"

"What have you got?" she repeated, drawing his arm from behind him. A bouquet of white daisies, their sun-yellow centers winking a greeting, flashed into view. Sarah's eyes rushed to his. "Oh, Cade," she whispered as her palm found the side of his cheek. "And I said you weren't romantic."

This time there was a slow, savoring tenderness to their kiss.

"Well, if you don't want to fool around," Cade said minutes later, "would you like a vase?"

"Does it have to be an either/or?" she teased.

"I'm quite willing to negotiate a both/and," he teased back. "Should I have my lawyer contact yours?" He gave a naughty wink.

Sarah was still laughing when he left the studio in search of a container for the flowers. The "vase" turned out to be the oversized beer stein she had first seen upon her arrival. And the daisies, which he had already arranged in the glass mug, could only be called rambunctiously displayed. Blossoms poked and peeked from angles that would have sent a florist into coronary arrest.

"You might want to do these over," Cade said, placing the beer stein on the desk.

"They're lovely," Sarah said, smiling at the disarray but knowing she wouldn't have rearranged the daisies for all the money in the world.

The flowers, the beer-stein vase, and Cade's thoughtfulness tugged gently, warmly at her heart . . . along with another feeling she couldn't quite identify. It, too, made itself felt as a plucking of her heartstrings, and it was a feeling as warm as a blazing winter hearth. For the rest of the day, it lingered, making her glance frequently at Cade, as if somehow another look would clear away the mist and put the emotion center stage. The evening meal came and went. The emotion grew stronger, more persistent, more potent, almost, *almost*, making itself known. It threatened identification when Cade massaged her tired shoulders, leaving behind kisses in place of soreness, but the emotion backed away like a tempting mistress when she showered and readied herself for bed. She had the feeling, though, that she was very close to some treasured discovery.

It came as Cade made love to her.

Gentle man-woman movements, silvery sighs, silken endearments, silent words that spoke louder than shouts, bodies tangled in love and laughter—all followed by rhapsodic sensations rushing, tumbling toward a culmination of light and dark, being and nonbeing. And in the rapturous, blissful afterglow came her heart's discovery.

She was in love with Cade.

As he slept beside her, his breathing a song in the night,

she wondered if she'd always been in love with him and was only now allowing herself to admit it. Whenever its beginning, she marveled at the admission, an admission that brought both joy and pain—joy that she loved him, pain that it might be simpler for her life, and his, if she didn't. Suddenly her heart constricted. Did he love her? She finally fell asleep only hours shy of a dappled dawn. Her last thought was that, even with all they'd shared, he'd never said he loved her.

Never.

The phone rang the next morning as they worked on the comic strip.

Cade, preoccupied with flipping through back issues of the newspaper, mouthed around the pencil in his mouth, "Catch it, will you?"

Sarah reached for the shrilling instrument as she put the finishing touch to Ms. Mona's broomlike eyelashes. "Hello?" she said with the delayed realization that she could easily be confronting David on the other end. A similar thought obviously jumped to Cade's mind, because his eyes flew to her.

There was a pause on the phone before a feminine voice asked, "Sarah?"

"Terri?" Sarah said, relief flooding her. Cade also visibly relaxed.

"Hey, Sis, whatcha doing?"

"I'm working. What are you doing?"

"Talking to my sister, who's obviously forgotten how to write letters."

"It's Terri," Sarah whispered to Cade over the covered mouthpiece.

He smiled and stood. "Tell her hi."

"Cade said to tell you hi."

"Hi, Cade," Terri Richards sang out in a bubbly voice.

"Hi, Cade," Sarah chanted to the man moving closer and angling his head. His lips brushed hers.

"I'm going to the kitchen for coffee," he whispered.

Sarah nodded, watching him leave the room, unable to

believe it had taken her this long to realize she loved him. It was so obvious to her now that it swirled her head and swelled her heart. "About that letter I've intended to write..." she said absently into the receiver.

"You okay?" Terri asked, a frown in her voice.

"I'm fine."

"You sound funny."

"I'm fine. Listen," she said, gathering her thoughts, "am I forgiven about the delinquent letter?"

Terri laughed, and Sarah could almost see long blond hair being flipped behind an ear. "Of course. I just wanted to hear your voice."

The two women chatted about friends and family, especially their parents, jumping at last to Terri's two children.

"How are my favorite niece and nephew?"

"Fine, if you like whirlwinds in the house. Denise just gave Daniel a haircut. I figure the hair will be grown back around the time he can get his driver's license."

This time Sarah laughed, but as always some unfriendly part of her mind told her that if she hadn't lost her baby, it would now be a little older than Daniel. She chased the thought away and forced herself to focus on Terri's smooth voice.

"So how's the job going?" she asked.

Sarah hesitated, not really wanting to tackle that subject either. "Great," she answered, edging the phone from one ear to the other.

"That's it? You're working on one of the best-loved comic strips in the nation, and all you've got to say is one word?"

"What do you want me to say? It's... it's... great."

"How's working with Cade?"

"Great."

There was a long pause. "Okay, what's wrong?"

Sarah changed the phone back to the other ear. "Nothing's wrong, silly."

"C'mon, Big Sis, I'm the woman you told when you let Brian Gilbert soul-kiss you."

Sarah smiled despite the fluttering in her stomach. "Lord, aren't you ever going to forget that?"

"No. I was livid with envy. Not about Brian Gilbert, but about being soul-kissed." Levity slipped away. "What's wrong, Sarah?"

Sarah paused, sighed, and sent up a silent prayer. "Cade and I . . . we're . . . uh . . . we're seeing each other."

"I would imagine so, working next to each other," the other woman replied, clearly confused.

"No, I mean . . . I mean, we're dating. Man and woman kind of stuff."

This time the pause would have filled the state of Indiana. Sarah's stomach twisted and twined until a ball of nausea lodged in her throat. It was the same silence she had heard when she'd first told her sister she was going to work for Cade. The same disapproving silence? Oh, Lord, she thought, here comes the real heartache. Mrs. Babish's criticism would mean nothing compared to her family's.

"For godsake, Terri, say something," Sarah begged.

"Look, will you just give me a minute to adjust? You did say you and Cade, didn't you?"

"I did."

"Dating, right?"

"That's right."

"Well, to borrow your word, I think it's great."

The knot in Sarah's stomach uncoiled slightly; she now felt only half sick. And more than half stunned. "You do?"

"I do. And I'm not really surprised. You and Cade were always more suited to each other than you and David."

"We were?"

"Well, of course, you were. And, frankly, I always thought Cade was crazy about you."

"You did?"

"Sarah, will you drop this bisyllabic conversation and tell me how serious this relationship is?"

Sarah swallowed hard, dislodging the knot in her throat, which then relocated in her heart. "I'm in love with him."

A low whistle. "That serious, huh?"

"That serious."

"Does he love you?"

"Lord, I hope so," she added, raking a swath of hair

from her eyes and adding, "What do you think Mom and Dad will say?"

"The truth?"

"Yeah. I think," she added belatedly.

"I think they'll be surprised, but I don't think there'll be a problem—at least none an adjustment period won't take care of. Speaking of problems, though," she added, "does David know?"

"No," Sarah said flatly.

Terri Richards made a noise that sounded like a deflating balloon. "I wouldn't want to be the one to tell him."

Long after the conversation had finished, Sarah stared at the phone. Her sister's comment nagged like a bad case of the flu. The truth was that she didn't want to be the one to tell David either. For that matter, she didn't want anyone to tell him. She had a heartsick premonition that David's knowing about her and Cade would herald the beginning of the end.

From a corner of the sofa, her feet folded beneath her, Sarah stared unseeingly at the crossword puzzle in her hand. The felt-tip pen she held hadn't made a single mark since she and Cade had finished dinner and settled down on the sofa. She had poised the pen for action several times, but her attention had wandered each time. The man at the other end of the sofa, his feet propped on the coffee table, his fingers curled around a suspense novel, was the reason for the breaks in her concentration.

She wanted to tell him she loved him. She'd wanted to tell him all day, especially after talking with her sister that morning, but the words wouldn't come. She didn't know why. Or did she? Bottom line, wasn't she afraid that her love wouldn't be reciprocated? She knew Cade cared for her—the two of them had always shared deep feelings for each other—but caring wasn't necessarily love. It wasn't necessarily that mysterious and special relationship that can exist between a man and a woman. She knew, too, that he was attracted to her, but attraction, even as consuming as theirs was, still didn't constitute love. What if his feelings were based only on a physicality that he'd one day work out of his system? Where would that leave her? Alone, she thought, glancing up at Cade with a horrendous pain slicing through her heart. Alone, without the man she loved.

Love, Cade thought. He didn't know how it was possible, but he was growing to love her more each day. He loved her so much now that it was a painful weight on his heart. If only he could tell her what he was feeling, he might lessen that wearying weight, but he was still afraid of rushing her. He couldn't run the risk of spooking her. Not when his whole future, at least a sane future, depended on having her at his side.

He raised his head, his gaze skimming the top of the book and finding Sarah. His heart burst into a million shards of joy. He loved everything about her. He loved her hair, her eyes, the way she smiled. He loved her laughter, the way she giggled when he bit the back of her neck, the way she held him, sometimes, he daydreamed, as if she thought he'd slip away if she didn't hold on tightly. And he loved the way she made love to him. Oh, God, he loved that most. He loved the way she held nothing back, the way her body came to him with need, the womanly way she begged him to satisfy that need. A painful thought clawed at his breath. What if this were only physical for Sarah? What if there never came a time when her heart was involved? What if he was destined to be her friend, her lover, but not her loved one? What if . . . He took a steadying breath, forcing himself to let go of the tormenting mind-beast. It was then he noticed the distracted look on her face. It was a look he'd seen there off and on all day.

"Hey," he called softly.

Sarah glanced up.

"Something wrong?"

She shook her head. "No. Why?"

"You've been a little . . . vague today."

"My mind's always a little vague," she replied with a feeble attempt at a smile.

He pursed his lips in a tease. "Yeah, I guess it is at that."

"Thanks," she said, jabbing him with her elbow.

"I'm only being agreeable." His smile widened for a brief moment before his tone once more sauntered into seriousness. "You're feeling all right, aren't you?"

"Sure," she answered, "I'm fine."

His eyes fell to the puzzle in her hand. "You're not going to work that?"

Her eyes dropped to the newspaper; she sighed and stretched, laying it and the pen on the coffee table. "Guess not. You're not going to read that?" she asked, sliding her attention to the book he still held.

He tossed the book, without even marking his place, onto the coffee table. It thwacked against the wood. "Guess not."

They stared at each other, both hearts so full of love they were miserable.

"Come here," he said roughly, pulling her to him and fitting her equally against his chest and into the crook of his arm. She stretched out her feet next to his on the table.

He felt so warm, she thought, carefully taking his injured arm and entwining their fingers. So warm, so masculine.

She felt so soft, he thought, his fingers tightening in hers, his toe skimming the bottom of her foot. So soft, so feminine.

"You have a hole in your sock," she announced lazily.

Cade held up his foot. A penny-sized hole allowed a glimpse of big toe. "They're not really broken in until they get holes," he said.

She angled her head up at him. They both smiled. Minutes of contented bliss eddied by.

"What! No new autographs?" she teased a short while later as she inspected his cast. "You mean you went into town yesterday without one new autograph from a female admirer?"

"You're still teed off about Bambi, aren't you?" Cade asked, unable to keep a smile from his face.

"Bambi who?" she said, her own face a study in earnestness.

"Yeah, you're teed off," he reaffirmed.

"To show you how un-teed off I am, Sterling," she said,

reaching for the felt-tip pen, "I'm going to sign right next to Ms. Bambi." Sarah uncapped the pen with her teeth.

"Definitely teed off," Cade said, loving the game they were playing because maybe it meant Sarah really did care. He was willing to allow himself the luxury of believing it for a minute, anyway.

Sarah positioned the pen above the plaster cast, her intent only to sign her name, but somehow, in those hovering milliseconds, her intent died and was reborn. What she ultimately wrote—with a trembling hand and almost as if she had no choice in the matter—had nothing to do with who she was, but rather with the condition of her heart.

Her heart. It was fluttering wildly. Oh, Lord, why had she just done that? Surely there was a better way! In contrast to her condemning heart, her brain told her that she'd at least guaranteed her passage from purgatory. She was on her way either to heaven or hell.

Cade tugged at the hand Sarah was suddenly holding fast. "Let me see that," he said, wrestling his hand from her grasp. "So help me, Braden, if this is an obscenity, I'm..."

When he saw the three words scrawled across the cast, his voice trailed off into obscurity. Emotions so powerful washed over him that he thought he was drowning in mountain-high waves. It crossed his mind to wonder if he were hallucinating. Had wanting something so long and so hard finally stripped away a layer of sanity?

At the sharp intake of his breath, Sarah eased from his arms and moved to the edge of the sofa. There she sat, staring at her folded hands but seeing nothing beyond the fact that she might have just made a colossal error. She cursed herself, she applauded herself for her courage, she waited . . . and waited . . . and when he said nothing, she wanted to die.

The sound came to her with the softness of twilight. It was the sound of breathing, shallow, uneven, fought for. It was the sound of low, long, but repeated swallows. It was the sound of weeping.

Sarah jerked her head up, her eyes meeting his. From eyes glassy with unselfconscious tears, he was watching her with an expression so unbelievably tender that she felt an instant prickling sting her own eyes. Her heart felt filled to bursting.

"Say it," he whispered, his voice wrapping her in a velvet cloak.

The moisture in her eyes swelled, and teardrops, fat and salty, rolled down her cheeks. "I . . . I love you."

He closed his eyes, and Sarah saw tears escape the fringe of his lashes. The tears ran unheeded down the hollows and angles of his face, a face that at that moment seemed more dear to her than life. And, strangely, Cade had never seemed more masculine.

"Do you—" The break in his voice forced him to stop and start over. "Do you have any idea," he asked, his eyes once more on hers, "how long I've waited to hear you say that?"

Her heart pounded; her eyes swam in an ocean of liquid hope. "I'm . . . I'm still waiting."

A tiny spark of disbelief darted across his face. "Surely, you know—"

"Say it," she interrupted him.

When he spoke, his voice was strong yet soft, a mixture of gray steel and pastel sunsets. "I love you. I've always loved you. Don't you know that you're my soul?"

As if he could wait no longer, he grabbed her, crushing her all along the length of him, pulling, clinging, almost hurtfully, to bring her closer, closer, and closer still. She cleaved to him with a strength that made her wrists ache, and yet she strove to draw him nearer, wanting, needing to lose herself in him. They cried, unashamedly and with the purity of lovers. Cade was first to stop, but he made no effort to stop her. He just held her and murmured pretty words of love.

"I love you," he whispered, bracketing her face and kissing one wet eyelid before moving to the other, where he again feather-kissed the pearls of moisture.

"I . . . I love you," she whispered, her hands trailing to thread through the thick hair at his nape. She sniffed and rested her cheek against his. Their tears merged.

His hands slid over her back in a motion of adoration that ultimately dragged her blouse from her navy slacks. With this freedom, his hands sought the warmth of her bare skin. He pulled her tighter, feeling her breathing as his own life force.

Slowly, Sarah stirred. She kissed the spot below his ear. He kissed a spot below hers. She kissed his neck. He kissed hers, moving unhurriedly though resolutely to the hollow of her throat even as his hands skimmed her ribs and traveled slowly upward. Her mouth found his, kissing him until a deep, lazy groan issued from his throat. His lips parted, pulling her willing tongue into the recess of his mouth. She moaned as his mouth tugged, forcing her tongue into a sensual simulation of love.

"Oh, Sunshine," he whispered, "is that what it feels like to have me inside you?"

"No," she said, her breath drowning in his. "Having you inside me is better. Much better."

When his hands, foraging beneath her blouse, found her breasts within thin bits of lace, she shuddered.

"Easy, love," he cooed. When he released the clasp of her bra, her breasts, as always, thrust forward to meet him. His good hand cupped her while his injured hand tried to. "Damn!"

"What is it?"

"I'm so damned tired of this cast. I want to touch you."

"Easy, love," she repeated with a tiny smile. She unbuttoned her blouse, slipping it and her bra to the floor. Lifting his wrist, she kissed each fingertip before lowering them to her breast, where she brushed herself gently against them—back and forth until flesh swelled and the nipple hardened to an ache. On a heavy siren's sigh, she closed her eyes.

She felt his breath warm against her breast, felt his tongue slide over the turgid tip, felt herself disappear into the cavernous moistness of his mouth. Soon all thought became as hazy as a morning mist on water's edge.

"Love me." It was a silken plea delivered in a gravelly rasp.

"I intend to," he whispered. "I intend to love my Sunshine by starlight."

Within minutes, the lamp had been extinguished, clothes had been scattered, and Sarah lay naked on the sofa. Cade, naked too, stood before her. Each watched the way stars and moon danced through the skylight, marbling bare bodies in silvery ribbons. A streamer of silver fell across Cade's chest, illuminating corded muscles and a sea of whorled hair. A banner of light drifted across Sarah's breasts and down, stopping only heartbeats away from the cradle of her womanhood. Cade, in silhouette, looked godlike yet sensually manlike—bold, powerful, yet possessed of breathtaking tenderness.

He was hers, she thought, hers in a way he'd never been before. He was hers in love.

She was his, he thought, in the way he had always known she was meant to be his.

She held out her hand; he took it and eased to her side. Gently, he kissed her lips, nibbled at her throat, her shoulders, her breasts. He crawled lower, grazing her belly, her thighs, at last slipping his hand between them to touch the wondrous essence of woman.

Both sighed.

"I can never quite believe," he whispered in a voice she could hardly hear, "that you're this warm and wet because of me. It's magic, Sunshine."

"You're the magic," she whispered, pulling him up over her and enfolding him in her arms.

He covered her, completely. He slid inside her, deeply. He made love to her, fully. Bold thrusts that robbed her of breath, slow rhythms that stole her sanity. Words, sweet and sensual, whispered in ears and against needing lips.

"Cade," she whispered, her hands riding the swell of his hips.

"What, love?" he asked on a ragged breath.

"Deeper," she entreated. "Until you're me . . . and I'm you."

He shifted her legs, angling her hips and arching himself as wholly as he could.

He groaned; she moaned. The world grew quiet.

Seconds stretched into minutes, minutes into more minutes, all measured by broken words and unbroken bonds. As the end neared, breathing shallowed, heartbeats scampered. Starbeams twinkled and glittered, while moonbeams swayed to the tempo of love. Sarah moved, arched. Cade answered in thrust and lift. Hurrying . . . hurrying . . . hurrying toward starbursts and shattering moons.

"I love you!" she cried at that special moment, clutching him to her.

"I love you," he growled, following only seconds behind her and clutching her to him.

The world spun far, far, far away.

Slowly, slowly, like brief wanderers in a perfect, enchanted land, they drifted back to an imperfect earth.

CHAPTER TEN

"OH, CADE, LOOK!" Sarah said the next morning as she flipped open the *Dallas Morning News* to the comic section. The crinkling of the newspaper overrode the rustling of bed sheets.

"I am," Cade returned lazily, seductively, following a night of lazy, seductive loving.

Sarah's eyes shifted to the man beside her. Propped on an elbow, his chest bare, his lower torso enticingly tucked beneath a sand-colored sheet, Cade watched her with eyes tinted a bedeviled shade of sultry.

"Not at me," she said, his blatant appreciation sending a thrill of pleasure scrambling over her body.

"Sorry, but I can't see anything but you. Do you have any idea how sexy you look in my sweat shirt?" Giving her no chance to answer, he leaned toward her, and Sarah caught only a quick flash of the sheet slipping to reveal an expanse of bronzed belly before his mouth captured hers.

With the merging of their lips, thought disintegrated into shapeless, erotic patterns. His tongue outlined her mouth and boldly slid between the silken seam of her lips to enter the heavenly warmth. On a blissful sigh, Sarah made the mental note to always wear his sweat shirt to retrieve the morning paper. She underscored the resolution when his hand eased beneath it and palmed the curve of her bare hip to draw her nearer.

"Now, what am I supposed to look at?" he whispered minutes later when his mouth released hers.

"What?" she breathed.

He smiled, pleased at her obvious disorientation. "I believe you wanted me to look at something."

"Oh," she said, a fragment of sanity returning. "'Rigby Rat.'" She pulled the paper toward them. "It's my cartoon. I mean, it's *your* cartoon, but it's the first one I drew. It's the one where you broke Rigby Rat's foot. Look." Her words were liberally laced with a novice's excitement.

"So soon?" Cade asked, glancing down at the strip.

"What do you mean so soon?"

"It usually takes about six weeks for a panel to make it into print." Cade laughed. "I'm sure this is my editor's way of teasing me about the wrist."

Sarah gathered up the hand under discussion, brought it to her mouth, and kissed the fingertips. "I've grown rather fond of if. Of course, I'm rather fond of all of the man."

"Are you now, Ms. Braden?"

"I am, indeed, Mr. Sterling."

"I'd make you prove that, but right now it's time to honor an age-old tradition in the cartooning world."

Her heart sprinted at the sensual smile nipping his mouth. "And what is this age-old tradition?"

"It's called the Ceremony of First Printing. Whenever you see your work in print for the first time, it's imperative that you observe certain rites."

A smile now tweaked the corners of her mouth. "And what are these rites?"

Sarah's smile broadened and her heart thudded as the sweat shirt was pulled over her head and carelessly tossed to the smoke-blue carpet.

"There's only one acceptable way to celebrate..." His words were lost as he slowly levered her flat on her back and imprisoned her mouth in a hungry kiss.

A short while later, the phone rang.

"Let it ring," Cade commanded thickly, caught up in the celebration of more than a first printing.

Sarah's answer was a moan of agreement.

In the background the phone rang and rang before it finally stopped.

Forty minutes later, the drizzling noise of a shower commingled with the sunny notes of human laughter and the low, unmistakable music of love talk.

From the bedroom, two furry muskrats listened with rounded ears, then, deciding the room was theirs, scurried from the pages of the Dallas Morning News *and scampered across passion-rumpled sheets to plop on fat, fluffy pillows.*

"Let me see," Ms. Mona ordered, reaching for Rigby Rat's front foot, which was as black as a spade and now bound in a cast the equal of his creator's. "Ah," she sighed, her wide eyes filled with caring, "your foot's broken." With great tenderness, she slurped wet kisses along the injured appendage.

"Ah, Mona," Rigby Rat chided, though, curiously, he made no move to pull his foot away.

"Thank goodness it wasn't broken last night," she added, ignoring his protestations, "or you'd never have been able to help her hold the pen as she signed the cast. Thank goodness—"

The phone rang.

Both heads jerked toward the trilling instrument. Fear suddenly whitewashed the room.

"Is it . . . is it the trappers?" Ms. Mona whispered, dread glinting in her dark eyes.

A knowing look passed over Rigby Rat's face. His attention shifted from the phone to the bathroom door, from which still came sounds of shower and laughter, then back to the phone.

"Of sorts," he answered sadly.

Fresh from their shower, Sarah watched as Cade ambled into the studio. His attention was lost in the bundle of mail

in his hand while her attention was blatantly cornered by
the virile way the white tennis shorts fit his body. It crossed
her mind to wonder if being in love unbalanced one's hor-
mones; it also crossed her mind to wonder if she, if *they*,
were going to get any work done today. She decided the
only chance of productivity lay in their working on separate
continents.

Cade glanced up and held out a letter. "Our favorite
neighbor," he said without a smile.

Silently, Sarah took the envelope, slit it open, and read
a blunt relay of her phone messages. Because of what had
happened, she hadn't been certain Mrs. Babish would forward her calls—indeed, this was the first time she had since
the embarrassing episode in Dallas. Despite the scene with
the woman, Sarah was pleased to have the information . . .
at least she was pleased until her eyes spotted David's name
printed not once, not twice, but three times on the list.

She felt that some of the magic of the last twenty-four
hours had just been snatched from her. Being in Cade's
arms, being tenderly assaulted by his protestations of love,
obliterated all concerns, all worries. But Cade was the dream;
David, the reality that the dream was riddled with problems.
She felt reality tightening a chafing noose around her neck.
She had just opened her mouth to tell Cade about the calls
when a loud whoop blasted from him and reverberated, like
wild gunshot, about the room.

"I don't believe it! They did it! They actually did it,
Sarah!" The letter in his hand sailed into the air and nose-
dived onto the desk.

Instantly caught up in an enthusiasm she could tangibly
feel but didn't understand the why of, she asked, "They did
what?" She frowned. "Who are they?"

"The toy manufacturers. They've agreed to the financial
deal I wanted." He rounded the desk and swooped her up
into his arms, twirling her around and around until both
were giddy with laughter. "Damn, we're talking mega-
bucks!" he cried as he slid her the length of him and settled
her feet back on the floor.

"And Ms. Mona?" Sarah asked, her excitement now as wild as his.

"And Ms. Mona," he confirmed with a broad grin.

Sarah's grin widened.

He hauled her to him again, squeezing her so tightly her ribs ached. He gave another satisfied shout. "Oh, Sunshine, I'm going to buy you the biggest diamond in Texas!" He instantly sobered. Sarah sensed his change of mood in the way his every muscle paused and slackened, in the way his breathing suddenly rushed past her ear in a rough torrent of air. Slowly, he pushed her at arm's length. "You will marry me, won't you?"

He wore his heart in a pair of summer-blue eyes that Sarah thought had never looked quite so beautiful, nor so appealing. They reached out to her, beseeching, tugging at her heart, until reality and its imperfections faded away to inconsequence. Only Cade mattered. Only Cade and his arms. Only Cade and his blue, blue eyes. Only Cade and his love and the heart-stopping question he'd just asked her.

"Yes," she whispered. "Oh, yes." As she moved back into the shelter of his arms, Mrs. Babish's letter, with David's phone messages, lay forgotten ... or at least buried far beneath the quiet wonder of the moment.

Sarah and Cade held each other, bound together with the strong silken ties of love.

"I love you," she whispered, her cheek nestled in the hollow of his.

His hold tightened. "I love you. Oh, God, Sarah, I love you so much, I—" He swallowed back a thick knot of emotion. "I love you so much, I can hardly believe you're mine."

"I'm yours," she breathed against the side of his neck, where she left a tiny moist kiss as if on an altar of worship.

"I used to lie awake at night wondering what it would feel like to ask you to be my wife and have you say yes." As he spoke, one hand tangled in her hair, while the cast lay a now-familiar weight on the swell of her hip.

She pulled back until their eyes met. "And what does it feel like?"

"There are no words for it," he said seriously, his thumb brushing the crest of her cheek, "in any language I know."

His head inched toward hers, and their mouths met in a total surrender of souls. What he couldn't say with words, he spoke with the feathery softness of his lips as they moved across hers. What she hadn't heard in words, she read from the supreme articulation of his touch.

The kiss ended. Their gazes locked. Both pairs of eyes shone with a thin layer of moisture.

"We're not going to cry again, are we?" he asked. He looked as though he could go either way, depending on her decision.

A smile started in one corner of her mouth; with the speed of lazy lightning it tripped across the fullness of her lips. "No. No tears."

And then, they were laughing and hugging and kissing and laughing again.

Suddenly he pulled back and said dubiously, "You're going to be Mrs. Sterling again. Will you mind?"

Sarah smiled. "This time I'm going to be Mrs. Thomas Cade Sterling."

He grinned in relief.

"And we're going to live here?"

"Yes," she answered.

"And you're going to help me with the strip?"

"Yes, if you like."

"I like," he answered. "And you can still free-lance," he added.

The phone rang just as she agreed. "Yes."

"And we'll be married soon?" he asked.

The phone rang again.

"Yes."

"And we'll honeymoon on some island resort that insists newlyweds stay in bed eighteen out of twenty-four hours?"

They were both smiling as if they'd just invented the state of love. "Yes, yes, yes!" she cried.

The phone pealed again.

"Why don't you get the phone while I see when I have to be back in Dallas. I don't want to miss this honeymoon."

He moved toward the desk and the letter, his mind on sun and sand and Sarah, while she reached for the phone, her thoughts on sun and sand and Cade.

"Hello?" she answered, her heart so light she was having trouble keeping it anchored in her chest.

There was a pause. A long pause.

"Hello?" she said again.

"Is this the Sterling residence?" came a male voice.

"Yes, it is. Would you like to speak—"

"Sarah?"

The heart that moments before had felt light instantly turned into a lead weight that pressed so heavily against her chest that it threatened to smother her.

"David," she said quietly.

Cade's head whipped up, his eyes clashing with hers. He gave a deep, agonized sigh and muttered, "Hell!"

"What are you doing in Gilmer?" David Sterling asked, not even trying to conceal his surprise.

"I'm . . . uh . . . I'm helping Cade with the strip." Her eyes were still on Cade, drawing from him what strength she needed.

"Oh. I see. How's it going?"

"All right, I guess. He hasn't run me off yet." Hoping to change the subject, she added, "How've you been?"

"Okay. I've been trying to get in touch with you." It sounded almost like an accusation.

"I know. I just received a list of my phone messages." Sarah's eyes drifted toward Mrs. Babish's letter. Cade's eyes followed; he dragged his hands to his hips and swore again.

There was a pause at David's end of the phone as if he were waiting for her to question why he'd been trying to reach her. When it became apparent that she wasn't going to accommodate him, he said almost irritably, "I'd like to talk to you sometime."

"Sure. I'd like that," Sarah lied. "Look, here's Cade now," she threw in quickly in what she would have readily admitted was the most cowardly act of the year. She heard David calling her name but ignored it. Instead, she held out the phone to Cade.

They stared at each other, both seemingly apologizing, both seemingly seeking guidance. Finally Cade reached for the phone and eased to sit on the stool. Sarah started to step past him, intending to leave the room, but he stopped and wedged her securely between his legs. He eased his mouth up to hers, kissed her briefly, and whispered, "It'll be all right."

Sarah rushed an equivalent prayer heavenward.

"Hi, David," Cade said, forcing a lightness to his voice which sounded just that—forced.

"Why didn't you tell me she was working for you?"

Cade would have bet money that was going to be the first question, but knowing it still didn't prepare him for an answer. He toyed with the truth; he toyed with a lie. He settled for a response midway between. "I haven't talked with you in a while."

"Is she the one you told me you'd just hired?"

Cade felt his back fit snugly into the proverbial corner. It was a damned uncomfortable corner. "Yes," he admitted.

"Why didn't you tell me it was Sarah? We had just been talking about her."

"At the time, it seemed best not to mention it," Cade said, answering the question with the honesty he knew was inevitable.

"Best for me or you?" David asked, his voice not quite unfriendly but not quite friendly either.

"What does that mean?" Cade asked, the words painfully tearing at his guilt because the question had been right on target. He felt irritation creep over him, aimed at himself *and* his brother. He also felt Sarah shift in his arms, and he pulled her closer.

A silence ensued before David Sterling finally answered with a heavy sigh. "Nothing. It means nothing. Listen, I just called to touch base and to see how your wrist is."

"It's mending," Cade supplied, aware of the strain in the conversation, regretting it, but knowing there was no help for it. "Why don't you come up next week?" he suggested. "We'll have lunch." And a long talk, he added silently.

"Yeah," David answered. "I'll do that."

"See you then, right?" Cade asked.

"Yeah, see you then." Cade had started to drag the phone from his ear when he again heard David's voice. "Cade?"

"Yeah?"

"How is she?"

How was she? Cade thought, his body aware of every feminine molecule contained within the fold of his arms. She'd never felt softer, she'd never smelled sweeter, she'd never felt more like the missing half of his heart. And he'd never wanted to make love to her more than he did at this moment.

"She's fine," he said, striving for a decibel louder than a whisper but succeeding only partially. He also struggled with another round of guilt. Again his success was fractional.

A hesitation followed, then a muttered "Good," and the connection was broken.

Cade held the dead phone for a moment before relinquishing it to Sarah, who slipped it back into its cradle. When their eyes again met, a thousand fears and doubts and hopes flowed from one to the other.

"Cade, I don't want to come between you and—"

"Sh!" he said, silencing her and pulling her back against his warm body. "It'll be all right." He buried his face in the curve of her neck. "I swear to God, it'll be all right."

It was what they both wanted to hear, what they both wanted to believe, and tucked in each other's arms, hidden in each other's hearts, they did believe it . . . almost.

The day crawled by. Both put up a brave pretense of working, but ultimately the charade wore paper-thin and they called it quits. They decided to go into town grocery shopping, but the scene was so domestic that it only seemed to amplify their problem. Once back in the van, grocery sacks piled behind them, Cade took her hand in his.

"Hey, will you stop worrying?" he chided seconds before a smile found his lips. "I don't want a worrywart for a wife."

His smile, and the word *wife*, proved irresistible, and

she joined in with a shallow smile of her own. "What *do* you want for a wife?"

His smile dimmed. "Not what, who. I want you. Only you."

She tumbled into his arms. "Oh, Cade, I'm scared."

"Of what?" he asked, holding her fast.

"Of losing you." It was an irrational fear she couldn't logically explain; she only knew it was tied in somehow with David.

"No way, love," he said, his lips brushing her forehead. "I've waited too long for you."

"But what if David—"

"Stop worrying, Sarah," he said firmly. "The two of us will have lunch next week, and I'll tell him everything. I'll make him understand. Now," he said, pushing her at arm's length, "will you stop worrying?"

She tried, but she couldn't. No more than she suspected he could. The telltale signs of worry were there in the way he stared quietly out the side window on the drive back home, in the way he studied the photograph of him and David and their parents, in the way he sat pensively nursing a beer on the patio long after they'd had dinner and she'd gone to bed.

When he finally came to her, easing in beside her with a body warm and aching with an immediate need, she offered herself to him.

"I love you," she whispered, her mouth sipping the malty taste of his.

"I love you," he breathed as his mouth and his hands flamed their bodies to the fiery pinnacle of desire. In haste, in a desperation they both shared, he moved over her, joining them in nature's wondrous design. Banishing worry, they loved, then fell quiet in each other's arms.

To sleep.

To dream.

To battle worry.

CHAPTER ELEVEN

"WHAT IN HELL is going on?" David Sterling hissed, shattering sleep and the peaceful morning in one fell swoop.

Both Sarah and Cade instantly and simultaneously bolted awake.

"What the—" Cade muttered groggily, coming to his elbows and adding the sharp, startled, "David!"

The word scattered the last foggy vestiges of sleep from Sarah's brain and catapulted her to a sitting position. Her eyes wide, her heart bounding from sleep-slow to pounding, she clutched the sheet to her bare breasts with a force that left her knuckles white. In contrast, a warm rose color crept across her face and neck.

"David!" she repeated disbelievingly, with the fond hope that he was only some nightmarish hangover from her troubled sleep. The hope went unrewarded.

"What's going on?" Cade growled, climbing from his elbows to a sitting position beside Sarah. He instinctively drew the sheet over her uncovered thigh and tried to shield her from view with the bulk of his body.

"That's what I'd like to know," David threw back. "What in hell *is* going on?" His eyes roved from Cade to Sarah and back in a carousel of insinuation. Each look elicited from the couple in bed a plethora of feelings: guilt, defiance, embarrassment, a slow-burning irritation—the last of which inevitably led back to guilt. "How could you?" David finally said into the awkward silence. It wasn't clear whether the question was meant for Sarah or Cade or both of them.

Neither answered. At last corralling some presence of mind, Cade said, "Look, David, why don't you wait in the living room while we dress? We can talk about this."

"You're damned right we're going to talk about it," he hurled back, but he made no attempt to leave the room. He simply stared, his brown eyes flashing, his features grim and hard and indicative of the emotions warring within him. He looked like a man on the edge of explosion.

"Please, David," Cade was forced to add, "give us some privacy."

Sarah was about to plead as well when David whirled on his heels and stalked from the room. Cade raked his hand through his hair, a disheveled mess from sleep and loving, and mumbled something foul. Sarah simply rested her forehead on raised knees and closed her sleep-gritty eyes.

"Oh, my God," she whispered into the sheets.

Cade angled his body toward her. "Are you all right?"

Her head jerked up, and the eyes that found his were glazed with tears of mortification. "I'm just dandy," she said, her tone scratchy with sarcasm. She instantly hated herself for her reply, but not enough to apologize. She was still too embarrassed. Still too mortified. Still too scared of what was about to happen in the living room.

Cade opened his mouth to say something, decided against it, and yanking back the sheet, slipped from the bed. Naked, he crossed the room and grabbed up a pair of jeans that lay crumpled in the corner. Not bothering with underwear, he rammed one leg into the denim folds, then the other, finally jerking them over his hips and zipping them in front with an irritated gnash of metal meeting metal.

"How did he get in?" Sarah asked, scooting to the edge of the bed and catching the robe Cade tossed in her direction.

"The front door, of course." His voice reflected the same curtness she'd just exhibited.

"Didn't you lock the front door?" she asked in exasperation, in accusation.

"Of course I locked the door!" he barked as he picked up a shirt and threw it back down. "David has a key. He *is* my brother."

"I know," she volleyed back, standing and jamming her arms into the sleeves of the cotton robe. She reseated herself on the bed. "That's the problem."

Cade drew a long breath as he planted his uninjured hand on his hip. He stared at the floor. Exhaling the long breath he had so laboriously sucked in, he walked to Sarah and squatted down before her.

"Hey, we're on the same side, remember?"

She, too, expelled a sigh. "I'm sorry," she whispered, her eyes dewy with apology. "I didn't mean to snap at you."

"I'm sorry, too." He pushed her trembling fingers from the buttons she was ineffectually trying to fasten and, one by one, closed her robe. When he finished with the last button, his eyes traveled back to hers. "We've done nothing wrong," he said. "Our only sin is that we're in love." His hand eased to cradle her cheek, his thumb teasing the corner of her mouth. She leaned into his caress. "I do love you, Sunshine."

"I know. The only problem is," she said with a sad smile, "you love your brother, too."

To this, Cade could make no denial.

An impeccably dressed David Sterling stood in the middle of the living room, his fingers wrapped around the silver-framed photograph of the Sterling family. He seemed lost in memories of happier times—memories of a smiling mother, a protective father, and an adoring younger brother. Sarah watched David, watched Cade watch him, and felt, like a palpable force, the pain thickening the air. David's pain. Her pain. Cade's pain. Especially Cade's pain, which had settled in his eyes and fogged them a gray-blue.

As if just sensing their presence, David glanced up, his eyes slowly traveling from Sarah in her robe to Cade in his wrinkled jeans and no shirt. Both defendants stood barefoot and barely daring to breathe. Turning and bending, David set the photograph, not on the mantel where it belonged, but on the cluttered coffee table. When he straightened, his eyes found Sarah, and he stared with an expression of some tender emotion that seemed totally at odds with his angry outburst of minutes before.

"You were always so beautiful in the morning," he said, his voice unsteady.

Sarah fought back the warmth tinging her cheeks and swallowed down the taste of bitter-sad memories, souvenirs of a marriage that now seemed shrouded in the deep, deep past. "David, don't," she pleaded.

"She is beautiful in the morning, isn't she, Cade?"

David's eyes meandered in challenge from Sarah to Cade. The two men exchanged long, hard, unbrotherly looks.

"Can't we be civilized—" Cade began.

"Isn't she?" the other man hurled across the room.

"Yes!" Cade flung back.

Sarah moaned and mumbled a weak, "Don't. Please, don't."

"And she always made such sweet love in the morning," David added, his mood swinging from tender back to hurtful. "Don't you think she makes sweet love in the morning, Cade?"

"David, please!" Sarah begged. Her knees suddenly melted into a jellylike substance, and she reached out for the back of a chair.

Cade threw her a quick glance before shifting his attention back to his brother. "I have no intention of answering that, and you know it," he said. Sarah could hear him striving to keep his voice even.

David laughed mirthlessly. "Well, hell, why not answer it? We're all *family* here, aren't we? And you did say you wanted to talk about this. C'mon, Little Brother, is she a good lay in the morning or isn't she?"

"Stop it!" Cade hissed, his command fanning the air like a dragon's breath.

Sarah, her head spinning, now eased onto the edge of the chair she had been clinging to. "Why are you doing this,

David?" she said in a desperate whisper. "Why are you purposely humiliating me?"

"He's trying to hurt me," Cade said, his eyes never leaving his brother, "not humiliate you."

An eternity shuffled by on leaden feet. Suddenly, David gave a tortured sigh. "I'm sorry," he said, turning away and staring at some nebulous point above the mantel. "It's just . . . it's just . . ." He whirled back. "Dammit! How could you do this?"

Pain tore at Sarah's heart, the same pain that cruelly ripped at Cade's.

"We never meant to hurt you," Cade said, his voice shaky but brocaded with sincerity. He slid the fingers of his uninjured hand into the back pocket of his jeans. "Honest to God, David, we didn't. It just happened." He swallowed back a surge of emotion. "It just happened."

The vulnerable catch in Cade's voice tugged at Sarah's emotions, drawing out all the tender, comforting instincts she possessed. She wanted to hold him, to crush him to her heart, to kiss him until his hurt, his guilt, melted in the flaming warmth of her love.

"I love him."

At the softly spoken words, both men directed their attention to Sarah. She glanced up at Cade, whose eyes had mellowed to the color of her voice, then back up at David. "I love him," she repeated.

Cade took a step toward her but forced himself to leave it at one. His restraint became a fourth entity in the room.

"You used to love me," David said huskily.

"Yes," she admitted. "Used to." But never with the totality she loved Cade, Sarah thought. Her love for Cade made her feelings for her ex-husband seem counterfeit and creek-shallow. Her feelings for Cade were precious, priceless gold; those for his older brother only the momentary glitter of a fool's metal. Oh, Lord, why hadn't she met Cade first? Why hadn't she loved him first?

"I want you back, Sarah." David's voice had lowered from husky to almost inaudible. "If I have to fight for you, I—"

"Don't," she pleaded, feeling her heart cramp into a painful knot of regret. "Even if I didn't love Cade—" She stopped, gathered her thoughts into kind words, and said, "We have no future. We share only a past."

She could see this truth washing over him and finally sinking in. "And it's you two who have the future?"

"Yes," Cade said, glancing at Sarah before shifting his attention to his brother. "We're going to be married." A long, harsh silence followed. "Please, David," he pleaded, "try to understand."

David laughed brusquely, while his hand tunneled through his hair in a fashion reminiscent of Cade. "Oh, I think I do." He looked from one to the other. "This is nothing new, is it?"

A sudden sick feeling hollowed Sarah's stomach. "What do you mean?"

"I mean you two spent a lot of time together even when we were married."

"That's absurd!" she cried at the same instant Cade threw out the warning, "You're way off base."

"Am I?" David asked, his eyes boring into those of his brother.

"Yes. And you know it."

"I know you were around an awful lot. Especially toward the last."

"What are you suggesting?" Sarah asked, unable to believe what she was hearing.

David ignored her question, adding in his conversation with Cade, "I know that at the time I thought Sarah was interested in someone else."

"You what?" she cried, now virtually ignored by both men. Even though his accusation startled her, on some subliminal level nagged the feeling that maybe David had sensed her love for Cade even though she'd carefully hidden it from herself.

"What were you doing, Cade? Holding her hand and—"

"Dammit, David, nobody would have had to hold her hand if you hadn't been out chasing every skirt in town! I couldn't even find you when she was losing the baby!"

The remark was sobering—to three people. Strong fingers of guilt gripped Cade by the throat; an old though unhealed wound was split open for Sarah; and David seemed to experience a blinding flash of anger.

"Well, maybe the right man was with her after all."

Sarah sucked in a gust of air at the implication of his words. "You can't mean—"

David's eyes nailed Sarah with a flaring intensity. "Was it his baby, Sarah?"

He took a step toward her; at the same time she stood, instinctively meeting her accuser head on.

"How dare you?" she whispered, tears springing to her eyes.

"Was it his baby?" David repeated, taking yet another step toward her.

"Back off," Cade said, the words vibrating with danger. "Use your head. If we'd been seeing each other, do you think we would have waited this long to get together?"

But David seemed incapable of using his head. "Dammit, was it his baby?" He reached out a hand, manacling her upper arm. She cringed. Cade grabbed his wrist.

"Don't touch me," David roared, wrestling free and stumbling backward. He bumped into the coffee table, sending the photograph crashing to the floor.

"Leave her alone," Cade threatened. "Just leave her—"

The words were dammed behind an implacable fist that unexpectedly but expertly connected with Cade's face. His head swung to the side, the sickening crack of knuckles meeting jaw merging with Sarah's screamed "No!"

And then the room grew end-of-the-world quiet. The quiet of surprise. The quiet of shock. The quiet of heartsick remorse.

The two brothers stared at each other, Cade disbelievingly dabbing at the trickle of blood oozing from the corner of his mouth; David just standing, wide-eyed, white as a pallid moon. Neither seemed quite certain what had just happened.

"Cade?" Sarah whispered. He made no move to acknowledge her; indeed, he and the man before him suddenly seemed unaware of her presence. The moment contained only brother and brother.

"I . . . I . . ." David stammered, contrition sweeping across his face as he absently rubbed his stinging hand. "I'm sorry," he finally managed to get out. Without another word, with only one backward, bleak look, he turned, walked from the room, and out of the house.

Cade said nothing, did nothing . . . except stare at the empty place where his brother had stood.

The moments stumbled by. Sarah's gaze never wavered from Cade. Cade's gaze never wavered from the spot before him. Finally, tentatively, with all the love in her heart, she stepped toward him.

"Cade?" she whispered.

There was no response.

"Cade?" she repeated, laying her hand on his forearm.

His muscles twitched as if her touch had startled him, and his head angled toward her, sharply yet vaguely. He seemed surprised to see her there.

"Are you okay?"

He nodded, grimacing at the pain the act obviously cost him. He felt his mouth once more with tentative fingers. "Yeah." He looked toward the front door, which David had just walked out of, then back to Sarah.

"Cade, I'm so sor—"

"It's not your fault," he cut in tonelessly. "Look," he said as he eased away from the hand on his arm, "I need some time by myself." His eyes probed hers a moment before he stepped away, his bare feet padding from the living room toward the kitchen. Within seconds, she heard the kitchen door close.

He was headed for the meadow. She knew he was headed for the meadow. It was where he'd gone before in time of stress. The meadow with its quiet solitude. The meadow with its comforting warmth. The meadow *without* her.

Sarah's heart shriveled inside her chest even as she rationally told herself that Cade's going to the meadow instead of turning to her meant nothing. He simply wanted to be alone to sort through what had just happened. But couldn't he have sorted through it with her? she thought, wondering if the coldness she was feeling now was what Cade had felt when she'd once refused his comfort. Didn't he need her consolation in a measure equal to her need of his? Didn't he need her arms? Her kiss? Her breath warm at his ear telling him that everything would be all right?

Dear God, she thought on a surge of panic, was he having second thoughts about their relationship?

"No! No!" she forced herself to say out loud, though the words that scattered the air had a strength of conviction that was lacking in her heart.

Suddenly, in a delayed reaction to the morning, the trembling started in earnest. She felt sick, she felt hurt, she felt . . . guilty. Oh, Lord, she felt guilty! she thought, hugging herself tightly so she wouldn't fall apart. So guilty! How had it come to this? How could something as perfect as the love she felt for Cade be the destructive force that had just caused one brother to strike another?

David had looked so stunned at what he'd done.

And Cade . . . Cade had looked so hurt. So betrayed.

Sarah inched toward the sofa and eased herself down. Merciful heaven, would she ever forget the blood seeping from Cade's mouth? Would she ever forget the look of his face blank with betrayal? Would she ever forget that *she* was the cause of the blood and the betrayal?

Her vision blurred, her hands shook, her stomach somersaulted. She cried. Because of the embarrassment of being caught in bed with Cade, because of David's unfair accusations, because two brothers had fought. Because 'Cade was now in the meadow and she was here, alone, on the sofa, crying and shaking and feeling sick at heart.

But mostly she cried because there was no way to change the fact that her loving Cade drove a wedge between two loving brothers, and she feared there would come a day when Cade would resent her for being that divisive factor.

She sniffed and wiped at the tears running down her cheeks.

But he said he loved her, she quickly told herself. And

she believed it. He loved her as David never had, as no man ever had, as no man ever would.

Because he does love you, the most loving part of her heart suddenly whispered, can you do this to him? Can you take from him the only real family he has? Haven't you always known the relationship was irreconcilable? Didn't you close your eyes to it the same way you closed your eyes to David's philandering?

Her eyes filled with a new flow of tears, and she raised the sleeve of her robe to stem them. It was then her eyes fell to the photograph. It lay on the floor where it had tumbled during the heat of battle. The Sterling family, happy and whole, stared back at her with a look that mocked, condemned, and branded her a stranger. The fall had broken the glass, leaving a lightning tear that slashed between the two brothers, isolating them one from the other, causing an equal tear to slash at her heart.

She reached for the photograph with fingers numb and cold and stared down at it through her smeared vision.

She could see two teenage boys standing shoulder to shoulder, smiling as if they shared some wonderful secret.

She could see those two boys growing to manhood, leaning on each other because there was no one else for them to lean on.

She could see those two men fighting, exchanging brutal words and hurtful blows. All because of her.

She could see the deadness that had entered Cade's eyes when David struck him. She could feel the infinite sorrow in his heart.

In the flash of a crystal-clear second, Sarah's own heart made a decision. Her emotions thankfully anesthetized by the reality of what she must do, she stood, walked to the bedroom, slipped from her robe and into her jeans, and quickly packed her personal belongings. She left a note, along with her heart, by the broken photograph. She then headed for Dallas. And away from everything that had meaning in her life.

* * *

The house still smelled musty, dust had again settled in rippled dunes, and the rubber plant had died a drooping, pathetic death. Sarah glanced around her vacantly, plopped down her things, and headed for the shower. Somewhere around three-quarters of the way home she had stopped crying and forced herself to admit that life went on, however much one would like it not to. She would simply turn to her job as a panacea. Even as she made this decision, she knew it was like relying on a Band-Aid when surgery was indicated, but it was all she had to bandage the gaping hole that had once been her heart.

Quickly, she showered and applied makeup to cover the ravagement of tears—she still looked as though she'd been crying—and dressed in a businesslike navy skirt and white blouse. With the haste of desperation, she phoned clients whose projects she'd completed and new potential clients from the recent list Mrs. Babish had sent.

You will marry me, won't you? Cade's voice haunted as she dialed the last number. Her heart turned over in her chest, and her eyes misted with a haze that blurred the phone.

"Hello?"

"Mrs. Allison?"

"This is she."

"Mrs. Allison," Sarah said, her voice so thick she had to clear it and start over. "Mrs. Allison, this is Sarah Braden. You left a phone message for me . . ."

Five minutes later, Sarah walked out of the house with a total of seven clients to see. While she knew it was unfeeling of her, she didn't care that all seven probably would have preferred something other than a Saturday conference. She didn't care; she was drowning, and they were her reeds of rescue.

At 5:15 Sarah looked down at her watch and wondered how, in the name of all that was holy, she was going to get through the last appointment. Working today had been a lousy idea. No, she amended, the idea had been sound; it was the execution of said sound idea that was lousy. She was drowning in a tidal wave of hurt so deep that there was no way these slender reeds could save her. All they did was offer her a mocking, ineffective haven from her constant storm of thoughts.

Cade. Cade. Always Cade.

Had he found her note—surely he had by now—and what had been his reaction? Had he been surprised? Hurt? Had he cried the way she had when she'd written it? Or had he been relieved that she'd brought a swift end to a painful problem? Was it a solution that he'd arrived at in the meadow? Had he concluded that they should go their separate ways, hurting awhile but realizing it was for the best? Or would he have thought that but never quite have had the courage to say so, instead staying with her out of love, out of honor, until love and honor were blighted by long years of isolation from his brother?

Sarah forced herself to end the painful speculation, parked the van, and headed for her last appointment with an attitude that bordered on despondency.

Mrs. Allison proved to be a gray-haired bank executive who had very specific ideas about what she wanted for the bank's new public relations project. With unspoken but heartfelt thanks, Sarah left after only thirty minutes. Only once did she make a fool of herself—which she considered something of a record for the day—and that was when she was caught staring out the window of the woman's plush condo. How long she'd been gazing out at the late afternoon sun streaking the sky she couldn't have said, but it had obviously been awhile, since the woman, concern in her intelligent eyes, asked if she was ill. Sarah had assured her that she wasn't and wondered what the woman would have thought if she had told her that she was remembering the way sun pooled through stained glass to leave its colorful pattern on bare skin.

By the time Sarah had stopped for gasoline and a carry-out hamburger she was certain would be "carried out" in the trash later, the sun was nodding an end to the day and shadows were beginning to grow a twilight gray. There were only two things in all the world that she wanted, she thought as she parked the van in her drive and threw open the door. She wanted a gin and tonic—heavy on the gin, nonexistent on the tonic—and she wanted to have another good cry. Not necessarily in that order, she admitted, feeling the sting of tears in her eyes as she plodded through the ticklish uncut grass and rammed her key into the lock.

She let herself in, sniffed, left her heels by the white wicker umbrella stand, and abandoned handbag and portfolio to the first handy spot she passed. She tossed the bag with the hamburger onto the counter and reached for a glass from the overhead rack. She threw in a couple of noisy ice cubes and covered them with the clear oblivion of gin. Moving to the sofa, she slumped down, eased her feet to the coffee table, and rushed a sip of the drink to her mouth. She grimaced. It tasted lousy—just the way she felt.

She exhaled a long, weary sigh and drove her fingers through her black hair. Oh, Lord, it had been only hours since she'd seen Cade, but already it seemed forever and four days. How was she going to make it without him? She lounged back against the sofa. Was he hurting as badly as she? Did he miss her? Was he right now nursing a drink and thinking of her? With her eyes closed, she brought the glass to her lips and took another strong swallow.

She had done the right thing. Hadn't she?

My Sarah . . . You were always mine . . . always mine . . .

Yes! she answered fervently. She'd done the right thing.

I can never not see your eyes.

She had to give him this option, she insisted. She *had* to.

I love you. I've always loved you. Don't you know you're my soul?

As badly as it hurt her, she'd had to leave.

I love you.

She heard the words delicately haunting her, felt their fiery brush at her ear.

I love you.

She felt his lips on hers.

I love you.

Felt him move deep inside her.

Love you . . . love you . . . love you . . .

Felt their passion-filled bodies gently, fiercely letting go to dance among the stars.

"Stop it!" she cried, jumping from the sofa and activating the answering machine. She stepped to the kitchen counter, praying there were a thousand phone messages to divert her mind, and poured herself another shot of gin.

A man's voice instantly erupted from the machine.

"Ms. Braden, this is Tom Hicks down at Black Ink Press. I've got that little job ready for you."

The message ended abruptly, followed immediately by another.

"Ms. Braden, Frank Ambrezzi here. Just wanted to tell you what a fine job you've done for me. 'Preciate it."

Sarah laughed, almost hysterically, at the irony of the moment. The two men who had just left messages were the same two who'd left messages that fateful day so long, so short, a time ago. Did nothing ever change? She swirled the clear liquid in the glass. Oh, yes, things changed.

"To change," she toasted lifelessly. She brought the glass to her lips, hesitated, and ended by dashing the liquid into the sink. Ice cubes thunked against stainless steel. She wearily set the glass down, gripped the sink with both hands, and dropped her head.

She had forgotten entirely about the answering machine. Until . . .

"Where in hell are you?"

Sarah's head jerked toward Cade's gruff voice.

"More to the point, what in the hell do you think you're doing?"

Sarah could almost visibly see him fighting for control. She could also see his fingers savaging his hair. She eased toward the salvation sound of his voice.

"I'm sorry," he groaned. "Sarah, I know what you're trying to do. At least I think I do, but . . . but this is no good. For us or for David. He and I h—"

The thirty seconds had played out. Her heart thumping, Sarah eased to the sofa and waited. Just when she thought her sanity was slipping, Cade's voice came back on—with a curse anyone would have considered indelicate. He took up right where he'd left off.

"David came back, and he and I had a talk. Everything's going to be all right, love. I promise. In time, it'll be all right. He's driving me to Dal—"

The message ended. Sarah waited, her heart now crazy-wild.

This time the thirty-second replay began with, "So help me God, I'll never leave another message on an answering machine!" Sarah heard him take a deep breath. "David's driving me to Dallas. We should be there before seven-thirty. All I want to hear when you open that door is that you love me. You got that?" She heard another sound filling the hesitation; she interpreted it as a long, unsteady swallow. "Unless . . . unless your leaving meant you were having doubts about . . . about us." She heard several deep, uneven breaths seconds before the tape went blank. She absently reached to shut it off. She checked her watch. Seven-ten. And she started to cry. Tears of relief. Tears of joy. Tears that lasted a long time.

She heard the shuffling of feet on the tiny front porch only seconds before the doorbell buzzed. She still sat on the sofa, from which she hadn't moved an inch since she'd shut off the machine twenty minutes before. She rose unsteadily and walked—she fought a run—toward the second impatient buzz. Turning the knob with a sweat-slickened hand, she opened the door.

It had been less than twelve hours since they'd seen each other, and yet each devoured the other as if unquenchably thirsty for some life-moisture only the other possessed.

Sarah's eyes roamed hungrily over the man illuminated in the golden glow of the front-porch light. He looked weary, with a dullness to his blue eyes that bespoke hours of stress. He looked expectant, cautious even, which the tight, thread-like lines at the corners of his eyes and fist-slit mouth attested to. And he looked as if he'd lost a sliver of his soul. It was such a subtle thing that no one else would have noticed—

no one except another person who'd just lost a sliver of her soul. His hair was mussed, his shirt and jeans wrinkled, his face puffy and purplish from the fight. He'd never looked more handsome!

Cade's eyes wandered greedily over the woman standing in the doorway. She looked tired, and she'd been crying. From the puffy redness of her eyes, it had been a long cry, maybe several long cries. She also looked . . . he settled on optimistically unsure. It was a feeling he could relate to. Her blouse was wrinkled, her hair disheveled, and her makeup in serious need of repair. She'd never looked more beautiful!

"Two questions," he said finally in a husky drawl. "David aside, are you having second thoughts? About us, I mean?"

"No," she breathed without hesitation. "Are you?"

He frowned. "Me?"

"You went . . . you left me and went to the meadow. I thought . . . I didn't know . . ."

He hung his head, raising it only after what seemed like a hellish eternity to Sarah. "I'm sorry. I had no idea you'd think . . . Sarah, I'm a loner when I'm upset. I always have been." He gave her a look filled with apology. "I don't think I can change. Even for you."

"I . . . I don't want you to . . . as long as I know . . ." She trailed off.

"Question number two," he added. "Are you in love with me? Do you want to marry me?"

It was two questions, but Sarah wasn't going to quibble away the moment with mathematics. "Yes," she whispered, "but—"

"But David," he interrupted.

"Yes."

"I can appreciate what you're doing, and if there were a Nobel Prize for nobility, you'd get it, but don't, please don't"—his voice trembled— "do this to us."

"I don't want to come between—"

"David and I are talking now. He's apologized for what happened this morning, and I've apologized for not telling him about us sooner. The road's rocky, but we're traveling down it. I think in time he'll come around. I swear to you,

I'll never stop trying to mend the break." His eyes darkened. "If the time ever comes, though, when I have to choose between the two of you..." His voice faltered, and he swallowed deep in his throat. "David's loss I could survive; yours, I couldn't."

Her eyes misted, overflowing the fullness of her heart.

His eyes misted, sky-blue and brimming with love and uncertainty and a thousand other wonderful, horrible emotions.

"Say something," he whispered finally.

"Kiss me," she whispered back, with a quick addendum of concern, "I mean, if you can, with your cut lip."

With a low groan that told her he could and would, he hauled her to him, strong arms banding about her and starved lips descending on hers. He kissed her harshly, uncompromisingly, and with a pain willingly borne. He ran a hand down to her hips, arranging her against him in a familiar fit as his tongue speared the sweetness of her mouth. All this he did right on her front porch, right under the glaring light, right before the eyes of God and Dallas.

At that precise moment, a car crawled down the street. Its pilot was John Babish, its copilot and commander-in-chief, Alma Babish.

"Look at that!" came her voice through the open car window. "Look at that! Of all the scandalous—"

"Oh, shut up, Alma," the retired drill sergeant barked in command. "Just shut up."

As the car passed by, Cade's head rose.

"I really think we ought to go inside," he said around breathing as thick as winter-chilled honey, "before I'm arrested for indecent exposure."

"I don't think anything's indecently exposed," Sarah answered on a flimsy fluff of air.

"Let's go inside and talk about it."

Sarah smiled.

He smiled.

They went inside.

And the discussion began.

EPILOGUE

IN THE MIDDLE of October the fans of "Rigby Rat" woke to a startling piece of news: Ms. Mona had at last caught her elusive lover and dragged him to a swamp altar. From the twinkle in Rigby Rat's eye, fans generally agreed—in fact, one morning talk show took to the street for reader reaction—that the force needed to drag him to that matrimonial altar was minimal. The same talk show host reported that, irony of ironies—or perhaps not so much an irony after all— the creator of "Rigby Rat," Thomas Cade Sterling, was at that very moment enjoying his own honeymoon. Three days earlier he had married Sarah Marie Braden. That she was his former sister-in-law was matter-of-factly mentioned only seconds before the newscast slid into an announcement of a prewinter storm invading the North Central part of the United States.

In contrast to the cold of the North Central states, a balmy breeze blew off the aquamarine waters of the Caribbean and traced its tropical fingers over the two sun-soaked bodies lounging lazily on the white sand of a secluded beach in Cancún, Mexico. The morning paper, containing the comic strip with Rigby Rat's marriage, fluttered under a bottle of coconut-smelling suntan lotion.

At the paper's languid rustling, Sarah's eyes drifted open. Peeking out from where her cheek was nestled in the crook of her right arm, her eyes strolled first to the gently flapping newspaper, then sauntered to her left hand, which was buried in sand and curled with Cade's. His cast had only recently been removed, leaving skin pale in comparison to the rest of his body—and leaving him with an insatiable need to always have that hand on her. She smiled drowsily.

Cade, lying on his stomach in a mirror pose of hers, his eyes closed to the peaceful serenity, tightened his fingers about hers. She exerted the same loving pressure.

Married. There were times during these past three days when she simply couldn't believe the truth of that. And yet, she knew it was true. The simple gold band on her hand, flanked by what might possibly *be* the biggest diamond in Texas, proved the point, as did the matching gold band on Cade's left hand. But, Lord, it was so hard to believe these kinds of forbidden dreams really came true. It was so hard to believe she possessed this kind of happiness.

Part of her happiness came from the reconciliation, shallow though it was at present, between Cade and David. The two brothers were trying. On the day of the wedding—an affair deliberately consisting of only Sarah, Cade, the minister, and the minister's wife as witness—David had sent a bridal bouquet of white cymbidium orchids and baby-pink roses, along with a note wishing them happiness. She and Cade interpreted it as an apology for the past and a peace-pledge for the future. It had been a lovely way to start their marriage.

At her side Cade stirred, shifted, and peeped from beneath sun-shuttered lids. "Wife?" he mumbled.

"Yes, husband?" she mumbled back.

"I've had about all of this sun I can take. Besides, it's almost siesta time."

"But I'm not sleepy."

As he released her hand and pushed to his elbow, his eyes traveled the length of her back—bare except for a minuscule string keeping the minuscule top in place— skipped lower to the flare of her hips projecting from black bikini bottoms so brief they wouldn't even wrap up the word *minuscule,* then skimmed lower still to perfectly shaped thighs, calves, and feet. He smiled lewdly. "That's what I'm counting on."

She fought back a smile but didn't even begin to fight back the delicious tremors that suddenly claimed her body. "And what makes you so sure I'd be interested in love in the afternoon?"

"What if I were to tell you," he drawled with all the confidence of an Adam to an Eve, "that I'm not wearing anything under these trunks?"

Like a cat sultrily stretching, Sarah shoved her weight to her elbow and let her eyes scan the length of his wide, furred chest and beyond to the tight blue swimming trunks allowing no doubt as to the veracity of his statement. "Then I'd say," she drawled with all the confidence of an Eve to an Adam, "that I'd definitely be interested in love in the afternoon."

With two hearts beating the same rhythm of promise, they rose and walked from the beach.

The seafront cottage, rustic and thatched, was shadowy with dim coolness. Cade clicked the door shut, leaned back against it, and immediately pulled Sarah into his sun-warmed and passion-heated embrace. She went without hesitation and in glorious anticipation. Their lips met in a fiery clash that bonded mouth to mouth, tongue to tongue, wet and warm to wet and warm.

"There's only one real reason I'm here," she whispered as the tip of her tongue slid along the moist surface of his bottom lip. "To make certain you don't fall out of bed. You have a history of doing that, you know."

"You'll just have to hold on tightly," he whispered back, taking her tongue into his mouth with a gentle, erotic suction.

Both moaned in exquisite pleasure.

Deft fingers untied the fragile decency of her swimsuit, and Sarah felt the snippet of material slither to their feet. His hands inched over her back, up her furrowed ribs, down to the trimness of her waist, moving forward to capture the

satiny fullness of breasts that seemed always swollen with
the need of his touch.

"You feel slick," he breathed, his hands kneading the
skin he'd earlier covered with silky lotion.

"You feel slick," she said, her fingers roaming over his
equally oil-sleek back and finally threading through the plush
brown hair on his chest. Fingertips raked across his male
nipples even as he found hers in a mind-destroying caress.
A ragged rush of air escaped her lips as the peaks pebbled
beneath his expert ministrations. His lips fell onto hers as
if he had no power to resist her reedy mating cry.

With the lack of preliminaries that familiarity allows, he
stripped the swimsuit from her hips, discarding his in the
process, and drew her across the room and onto the bed.
She rolled onto her back; he tumbled atop her. He took her
mouth again and again, sweetly, savagely, while both his
hands and hers moved over flesh in a never-tiring pattern
of give and take, tease and be teased, please and be pleased.
She touched all the places male to him—places hard and
straining and aching for her softness—while he caressed
all the places female to her—places soft and yielding and
longing for his hardness.

"Cade?" she whispered.

It was only a scrap of sound, but he heard it and raised
his head from the honeyed diversion of her body. Her hips
and legs were trembling and arching for the lovemaking that
was so close at hand. He noted this and the passion in her
beautiful gray eyes. But he saw in those crystal depths
something beyond passion. He saw a love so pure, so hum-
bling, he could only feel the vast inadequacies of his being.
He had never been, nor would he ever be, loved this way
again.

"What is it, love?" he whispered.

Her hand reached out and touched the strength of his
shoulder as if verifying his presence. "I'm not dreaming
this, am I?"

The question was so very much the same one taunting
his mind that under any other circumstances he would have
laughed. But not now. Now he could only shake his head.

"I don't think so," he breathed thickly, his body slowly shadowing hers. "If you are, Sunshine, I want to stay trapped in your dream forever."

With a tenderness that brought a glaze of tears to her eyes and a flooding warmth to her heart, he joined them . . . man to wife, lover to lover, forever-dreamer to forever-dreamer.

Somewhere in the world of make-believe, where dreams and reality have no boundaries, two muskrats stood watching the seafront cottage.

"Ah, love," Ms. Mona sighed, her thick black lashes crescenting her cheeks, her hand, laden with a clover-ring of muskrat marriage, going to her ample bosom.

Rigby Rat smiled at his furry bride. "Didn't I tell you we'd write them a happy ending?"

Ms. Mona smiled back, adoration in her dark eyes. "And will it last? This love of theirs?"

"Yes," he answered without hesitation, "for you see, of all the species, human beings are capable of the greatest love. And some few human beings have the capacity to love beyond eternity."

"Ah," Ms. Mona said, "how very interesting."

"How wonderfully human," the wise male muskrat replied.